CAN I HAVE A HORSE?

"You're asking for a riding horse?" dad said. "Now? At tax time, planting time, repairing time?"

He was getting louder with every word. Cassie couldn't answer again, or nod.

"If there's one thing we *don't* need," he thundered, "it's another horse. We don't need one more thing that can't pay its way." He banged his fist on the table. . . .

A Horse For Cassie

Jeanne Hovde

For Peggy and Penny
and every other young girl who ever wanted a horse

A White Horse Book
Published by Chariot Books,
an imprint of David C. Cook Publishing Co.
David C. Cook Publishing Co., Elgin, Illinois 60120
David C. Cook Publishing Co., Weston, Ontario

A HORSE FOR CASSIE

Previously published as *A Horse Named Cinnamon*
First Print, 1982
Printed in the United States of America
93 92 91 90 89 4 5 6

Library of Congress Cataloging-in-Publication Data
Hovde, Jeanne.
A horse for Cassie.
(A White horse book)
Previously published as: A horse named Cinnamon.
Summary: A girl who lives on a farm that has working horses tries different schemes to get a riding horse.
[1. Horses—Fiction. 2. Farm life—Fiction]
I. Title.
PZ7.H824Ho 1988 [Fic] 88-7355
ISBN 1-55513-587-0

Contents

1
A Horse For Cassie

It was spring, the first warm day of April in northern Wisconsin, and, shoes and socks in hand, twelve-year-old Cassie Andrews sailed in glee from the confines of the afternoon school bus. Her green eyes sparkled, and dark hair flew high behind her.

''Cassie, your books,'' someone shouted.

''Get 'em Monday,'' she sang, and hitting the ground ran ahead of Patsy toward the house and the bedroom they shared. Patsy was her twin sister. Everyone said she was a dead ringer for Cassie, but Cassie knew better. Patsy could sit still.

''Mom,'' Cassie called, throwing open the door, but she already knew the house was empty; the car was gone. Of course, Jess, her brother, would be somewhere on the place, but most likely at the barn or in the woods nearby.

Inside, Cassie smelled dinner in the oven. There was always an oven meal when mother was gone. Her nose hinted at scalloped potatoes and ham, but she didn't take time to check. Right now other things were on her mind.

A few steps took her down the wood-paneled hallway to the bedroom. Tossing her school clothes aside, she pulled on her old, blue cut-offs and her orange shirt with the paisley butterfly sleeves and plopped her soiled yellow visor on her head. It was the kind that couldn't be washed or the brim would collapse, but Cassie didn't care—it kept the hair out of her eyes. As she raced outside, Patsy was just coming in.

"Hurry up," she called. Then leaping from the porch to her lime green bike with the banana seat, she pumped to the corral fence and prepared to make one more attempt at friendship with Stampede, their big, Belgian draft horse. Cassie hopped on the offset rails with a handful of grass.

"Stampede," she called looking around. At first she she only saw Lightning, Stampede's yearling colt.

Then, alongside the shed, the better-than-a-ton sorrel greeted her as she always did, with one defiant hoof pawing the ground.

"Why do you insist on that?" Cassie asked for the thousandth time. "I only came to bring dessert." She held the offering over the top, but it was no use. Stampede danced a few smart steps, lifted her tail high, and tossed her head to send her blond mane flying. Then, whirling her broad back end, she pounded off to the far corner.

Cassie shook her head. Never before had she met an animal that refused to be her friend. Yet, despite the rebuffs, she liked Stampede. She was a horse. If only she were a riding horse.

But before Cassie could think further, a familiar green car turning in the drive caught her attention—the fat salesman who had been at the house yesterday and the day before that. Cassie remembered because his little car rose on its springs when he stepped out and squished down when he got back in. He braked, and the car quivered as it settled in place.

"Your dad around?" he called without getting out. Cassie didn't answer, for right then Patsy came from the house and was closer.

"He must have gone to town," she said, "but you're welcome to wait."

"Thanks," he said, "I'll sit right here."

Patsy left him and jumped on her bike. It was like Cassie's, only lavender with a big white flower on a purple seat. Cassie curled her bare toes around the middle rail and waited. As soon as her sister was alongside, she turned to face her.

"It's your turn to ask this time."

Patsy wrinkled her whole face. "You're better at it than I am."

"I asked for the bikes."

Patsy shook her head. "*We* asked for the bikes. *You* said, 'Dad, can we have a bike?' and *I* said, 'She means *two* bikes.' Besides, you want a horse more than I do, and asking for the bikes was easier too. We were little then and cute. Look at us now. We're not even beginning to take shape."

''Who cares?'' Cassie said.

''Celine does.'' Celine Finette was their friend and classmate. She was the only child in her family, and she had everything, including a horse.

''But we don't have to ask Celine,'' Cassie said. ''Dad's the one, and anyway, we don't need two this time.'' Not that one horse would be ideal, but she and Patsy were both small. Any size horse could easily carry them both. Besides, they were used to taking turns and sharing. And if they had a horse they could go riding with Celine who had been pestering them lately to ask for one.

Her sister sighed a long sigh. ''But we've been trying for two years already, and we still don't have a horse to ride.''

''Before now we probably couldn't have taken care of one,'' Cassie said, ''not right, anyway.'' She leaned forward. ''Besides, this is the time for a horse, right now, in spring.''

''Spring doesn't make any difference,'' Patsy said.

''But it does.'' Cassie knew she was right because of what mother had said last fall when out of the clear blue Celine got her horse and came over to show him off. She didn't prance the mare around long, only up and down the drive a few times, but the horse was beautiful enough to fill Cassie with both envy and admiration. Then, without even offering Cassie a ride, Celine rode off to see Mary, another girl in their class. As Celine left in a clatter of hooves, Cassie remembered running into the house to watch from a window with a clear view of the road.

''Look at her go,'' she said. ''It must be pure heaven.

I wish we could have a horse.''

Her mother hadn't said anything as she continued wiping the appliances. Quickly Celine and the mare were out of sight, and Cassie was left to face the counter heaped with another load of clothes from the dryer. She picked through the items, folded a pair of underwear, and the dryer quit again.

''All we get is another load of clothes.''

Her mother had quit wiping then, and picked up a couple of towels.

''It's fall now anyway,'' she said. ''You wouldn't get much use from a horse in winter. Spring would be the best time for a horse.''

Cassie remembered how her heart had given a little leap when she heard that—*spring would be the best time for a horse.* Oh, she knew it wasn't an outright promise, not at all, but to Cassie it was nearly as good. For that was the way things always started with mother. Just a little inkling, but whenever that happened, eventually the thing came to be. And now it was spring. Yet Cassie didn't think Patsy would put much stock in that reasoning, so she was trying to think of another argument when she felt a little nudge at her hand. She whirled around. It was Lightning nibbling at the grass she held.

''Lightning,'' she cooed, swinging one leg over the fence and reaching to stroke his soft, silky nose. The young stallion nudged her again, and Cassie opened her hand to give him the grass. Lightning was 16 months old, lighter in color than his mother, but with the same white splotch above the eyes. Cassie had worked with him a short time last summer. Stampede had been taken to be bred and he was alone in the corral. Now Cassie thought she wouldn't mind trying again. She took hold of the green halter and nodded to Patsy. "Pull some more grass. Then get the rope."

While Patsy scrambled from the fence, Cassie scratched around the colt's ears and kept talking. "It's been a while since we tried this. I bet you're anxious."

Lightning kept reaching for the grass. He was still smaller than his mother, but he was far more friendly. Of course, he had always been at the Andrews' farm.

In a minute Patsy was back. There was a small loop on one end of the rope, and Cassie tucked the other end inside to make a second. The small one she put over Lightning's lower jaw, and the larger one behind his ears. She pulled it tight and hopped into the corral.

Even leading a horse felt good. When she wanted Lightning to stop, she said, "Whoa," and quit walking. If he didn't understand, she pulled on the rope.

"Not bad," Cassie said when he responded correctly. "Not bad at all." But she stayed on the near side of the corral, and Stampede kept her distance.

They walked around a while, and Cassie felt pleased. Lightning tried to do all she wanted, and right then she'd have given anything if he wasn't a workhorse, but she didn't want him to know. He couldn't help what he was. Yet Cassie couldn't stop thinking of her real love, a fleet-footed animal who could pace with the wind, one to share her eagerness for every turn in the road, and, with her, streak toward it. Her horse would have slender legs, small delicate ears, and a flowing red mane falling on a sleek, shining coat the color of dark honey, or cinnamon. The very thought made her whole body tingle all over.

But the more Cassie imagined fleeting hooves and boundless strides, the more heavily plodded the weighty steps behind her. Finally Lightning gave her a nudge that almost knocked her down, and Cassie hurried back to Patsy at the fence.

"I'll ask," she said. "I'll ask tonight."

2
Bad Timing

Cassie was still in the corral when her mother and father drove in. She had forgotten they might return soon, and she tried to duck behind the rails, but dad saw her. He parked at the garage and jumped out.

"Cass," he called sternly, "get out of the corral."

"I'm coming," she said straightening up, but she didn't see any particular danger. Stampede was far away on the other side. She began loosening the rope when she saw Jess on the drive between the barn and the old stone milkhouse. He was coming toward them.

Her brother swung along with the same steady gait he always had, whether he was going three steps to the garage or out to the back forty. It made him look sturdy as a rock, as if, even if he had a hundred miles to go, he'd be sure to get there. His red hair glistened in the sunlight too, especially where it curled up at his ears, and the growth on his face was just enough to call a beard. As he neared, Jess left the drive and walked to where she was standing.

"In trouble again, Cass?"

"I'm not in trouble," she said, "I'm in the corral." Jess was a great guy, except when he teased.

"I didn't mean anything." Her brother stepped on the bottom rail, took hold of the halter, and stroked the big neck. "Trying Lightning again?" Cassie knew he didn't mean to upset her. She handed over the rope and nodded.

"And he was doing OK too. Last summer was a long time ago, and even then it was only for a few weeks."

Jess eased the rope from Lightning's jaw, ran his fingers under the straps of the halter, and gave the horse a real once over. "He's growing fast—don't want it too tight. Beautiful animal, isn't he?"

"If only he was a riding horse."

Jess smiled a little, gave Lightning a tap on the flank, and watched him trot off to the feed bunk. "Another if. Life is full of those."

Cassie knew what he meant. She gave one last sigh, turned, and climbed over the rails. She saw that dad and the salesman were in the house, but mother was still gathering bundles from the car. Then the car door slammed, and mother called.

"Come right in. Dinner is ready."

"I'll take the rope." Jess said, winding it in a neat coil around his arm. "You bring your bike."

"Thanks," Cassie said, and jumped on her bike again. When she reached the porch, dad and the salesman were standing inside the door. She opened it and slid past them to the kitchen, but stayed near the doorway so she could listen—and see too. The salesman was pointing to a page in his looseleaf binder.

"You won't find a better constructed unit anywhere in the country, Mr. Andrews. And the shed will pay for itself. It's proven right here on the paper."

"My figures turn out differently," dad said. He was taller than the salesman, but not nearly as heavy. His plaid shirt, open at the neck, looked a lot more comfortable than the collar and tie the salesman wore.

The salesman flipped a page. "Look at this graph, Mr. Andrews. You're at the break-even point right now. With just a little more grain. . . ."

"But I don't have a little more," dad said. "In case of a crop failure, I'd have even less, and I can't afford another thing that won't pay its way."

"You wouldn't be out a cent, Mr. Andrews. The shed could store machinery 'til the crop came in. I can guarantee financing." The salesman leaned forward. "Mr Andrews, you can't afford to be *without* this shed."

A funny look crossed dad's face. He put one hand in his pocket. Cassie shrank from the doorway and slid to the far side of the kitchen. Poor dad, being pressured that way. It didn't sound pleasant. If only she could wait. But there was Patsy waiting for her to ask, Celine with her own mare, and it was spring, the best time for a horse. Besides, something inside pushed her to have that horse, some threat that life itself would pass her by without it. She slipped to the refrigerator to skim cream from the milk and set it at dad's place. He always liked good cream in his coffee.

Cassie glanced over at Patsy, but when their eyes

met, Patsy looked away, and Cassie knew what she was thinking. Her own stomach didn't feel too good either. Still, she placed the cream pitcher near the sugar bowl and took her chair next to her father's. The door squeaked, and she heard the salesman's voice.

''Maybe next year,'' he said.

''Maybe,'' dad said, but it didn't sound much like a maybe, more like a no. The door closed and dad came to the kitchen. He sat down, but he didn't ask a blessing. Breathing hard and rubbing his forehead, he just waited a minute. Finally he rolled his sleeves once more and picked up the salad bowl. Mother bowed her head, and Cassie did too.

''Please, God,'' she whispered, ''let him say yes.'' She reached for the coffee and started to fill his cup.

Her father raised his hand. ''None for me, thanks. My nerves are on edge now.''

Cassie didn't say anything. She put the pot down, but she wished she was sitting across the table. It seemed it would be easier to ask from there, where she could see dad's face without turning. *Maybe I'll ask with my head down,* she thought, the way Patsy's was across from her, her eyes glued to the plate. But that didn't seem the right way either. If you wanted something bad enough, you ought to be willing to stand up and say so. Yet she was reluctant. Everyone was so quiet.

Finally dad spoke. ''Hear anything from Harold?'' he asked. Harold was Cassie's brother too. He was a year older than Jess and had started college right after high school whereas Jess stayed to farm when he graduated. Harold was OK too, but he was different, always in a hurry. Even when he was around home, he was off to every job he could find away from the farm.

Jess put his glass down. "There was a letter in the mail. His classes are going OK. Expects he'll have enough credits to go back as a junior. Says that puts him on the downhill side."

That seemed to make dad feel better. He eased back in his chair and looked a little pleased. "That's Harold. Always knew what he was after and went straight for it. You have to give him credit. Going summers too. It's been rough, but he'll make it." He reached for the potatoes and turned to Cassie. "Maybe I'll have some of that coffee after all. And I hope you saved some cinnamon rolls for me." He winked. It was a family joke how much Cassie liked cinnamon rolls.

Cassie reached for the coffee pot, and her spirits perked too. Now was the time to ask, when dad was thinking of Harold, but before she could speak, her father turned to Jess.

"Made up your mind to buy that forty yet?"

That made Cassie cringe again. She couldn't ask when he was talking about the forty. It was the land adjoining the Andrews' farm and owned by old Mr. Westin. For months dad had been after Jess to buy it.

Jess waited a little while before he answered. "Not really," he said.

Dad looked over his forkful of meat. "Good land, near the river, and not a handful of rock anywhere."

Jess didn't say anything further.

"You've got the down payment," dad said.

Jess still didn't say any more. He did nod a little.

"The price is right."

Cassie wiggled in her chair. She didn't like Jess being pressured either. Her brother took a mouthful of beans, and dad quit eating completely.

"Don't *you* think it's a good buy?"

Jess didn't look comfortable at all. He popped more beans in his mouth. "Probably is," he admitted.

Dad put his fork on the place mat. "And you *still* haven't made up your mind to buy?"

Right then Cassie couldn't stand any more. She knew it wasn't the time to ask, and she didn't know what made her do it, but she held up her head and blurted straight out, "Dad, can we have a riding horse?"

3
The Trouble with Stampede

Dad's mouth fell open wide enough, Cassie thought, that if he'd had false teeth, they'd have gone to the floor. She didn't look at Patsy.

"A *what*?" her father asked.

"A riding horse," Cassie squeaked, pulling all the voice she could find to make sure it came out at all.

"A riding horse?" he repeated.

Cassie couldn't say it again. There was no squeak left. She did manage a nod, but it was like signaling a volcano on the verge of eruption.

"You're asking for a riding horse?" dad said. "Now? At tax time, planting time, repairing time?" He was getting louder with every word. Cassie couldn't answer again, or nod. "If there's one thing we *don't* need," he thundered, "it's another horse. We don't need *one more thing that can't pay its way.*'' He banged his fist on the table.

Cassie felt a big steel door clang shut between them. Stinging tears filled her eyes. She tried to hold them back, stay at the table and keep eating, but the tears wouldn't stop. They spilled down her cheeks, and jumping up, she ran from the table and outside. The front door slammed behind her.

''Oh, God,'' she cried, running across the garden plot to the basswood tree, ''do you know what it's like to be twelve? Do you *really* know?'' Cassie knew, and it was torture. It was being too old to kick and too young to explain, too old to bite and too young to insist. It was dangling from nowhere, balancing on the top rail and knowing you'd fall. Which way, you couldn't be sure, but either way, it made you a fool. ''Do you really know?'' she called again. By that time she had reached the tree, and, curling her toes in the wound of the old leaning trunk, she ran all the way up to her branch of solitude. She cried for a while, loudly at first, then softly, then loudly again. *Why,* she asked over and over, *why can't we have a horse?* And she couldn't answer.

Finally Cassie calmed down a little. She blew her nose and propped her head against the next branch. Oh, she knew it had something to do with Stampede, and for just a moment she almost hated the big animal, but not really. Yet she did know that before Stampede came, dad hadn't been against them having a horse. ''When you're old enough to take care of it,'' he always said. Then he bought Stampede for one specific purpose, to skid logs on hills too steep for a tractor. He was so proud the afternoon he brought her home.

"Look at those muscles," he said. "You can see she's accustomed to work. Gus Soltis, the bachelor who owned her, showed her all over the midwest and Canada in an eight-horse hitch too. Won a lot of prizes."

Cassie liked the horse right away. She liked the way Stampede's mane fell to the right. She liked the longer, lighter hair around the hooves and the way the horse pranced when she walked with her head held straight and shoulders rolling rhythmically forward. Cassie liked the sound of her hooves hitting the driveway and the strong horse smell that met her nostrils. She even liked her name, Stampede. It sounded strong and wild.

"How much did she cost?" Jess asked.

Dad didn't answer right away. He wasn't nearly as tall as the Belgian, but he stood on his toes and brushed her mane into perfect place. He turned her head too, and she raised it, striking a pose.

"Plenty," he said at last, "but she's worth it. The foal she carries will sell for a thousand when dropped. Gus said so."

Jess whistled through his teeth and took hold of the halter on the other side.

"*If* it's a filly," dad added, "and a trained mare like Stampede. Well, that's unbelieveable." He paraded her around for the others to see. "Besides," he continued, "on the slim chance she shouldn't work out, I can return her. Money-back guarantee. Mr. Soltis said so."

It was perfect that far, but then. . . . Well, the mare hadn't worked out. The next day, with little more than an hour in the woods, she came thundering home unattended. Her eyes were wide, her nostrils were flaring, and the singletree and harness traces were bouncing along behind her. A neighbor stopped her just before she hit the fence.

The following day, Jess, dad and the horse came back together, but dad was limping. He was covered with mud and leaves, his shirt was torn, and he was scratched and bruised in some places and bleeding in others. Stampede had pulled two logs over him lengthwise. He went straight to the phone to call Mr. Soltis.

''There's no controlling that beast,'' he said to mother as he dialed. He was still shaking. ''No easy start, no respectable stop. She hits a load with that crazy prance, takes off, and won't stop 'til she's ready. I don't know what's wrong with her. She's going back today—right now—before somebody gets killed.''

Cassie was frightened. She waited at the table with mother, but when dad came back from the phone, he looked even worse, like a man who'd been beaten and kicked in the stomach besides.

''It's too late,'' he said, sinking into the first chair he came to. ''Soltis died last night. Heart attack. *That horse is mine*.'' He buried his head in his hands on the table.

That day Stampede was put in the corral, and there she stayed. Oh, Jess put her in the barn every night and out every morning, but whenever he tried to do anything more, dad immediately found something else terribly important for him to do. Cassie wasn't allowed in the corral either. She pulled grass and brought apples, but Stampede didn't coax easily. Mostly she pawed with that one big hoof. Dad had eyes like a hawk too.

Any time he saw her near the corral he came down with a foot as heavy as Stampede's. So the harness collected dust in the shed.

When the foal came, it wasn't a filly. It was a stallion, and after that, any time Cassie asked for a horse, dad clammed up. He just put his lips together and wouldn't say a word, until tonight. Then he'd said plenty.

Cassie straightened up, blew her nose, and wiped the last tears. She still couldn't see what all that had to do with her. It wasn't her fault, or anyone's. It was just something that hadn't worked out. She was thankful for the old tree—at least there was a place to be miserable—and for free feet. Scraping them against the rough bark felt particularly good after they had been cooped up all winter.

Cassie stayed in the tree a long time. Finally she saw Jess come to take Lightning inside. She climbed down, slipped to the fence, and was waiting when he came back. She helped him get Stampede in a corner. Finally he had her by the halter.

"Why won't dad let us have a horse?" she asked.

"I'm not sure, Cass." Jess looked at her and at the big Belgian. "I do know this was a financial loss, a stiff one."

"Can't dad make it up, sell her maybe?"

"Not as a trained mare. Not for what he paid for her. You know how she acts."

"But there must be some way. What about Lightning?"

Jess shook his head. "A stallion isn't worth much. With a filly, it's different. They have value from birth because they can be bred and give you more horses.''

Another colt! That was it. That was the answer. ''I know,'' Cassie cried. ''When she foals again.'' She raced ahead to open the barn door. Stampede had been bred last summer and the foal was due soon. Maybe it would be a filly!

4
The Prize Horse

Cassie flung the door wide. "Dad can sell the new foal, get his money back, and I can have my horse." She whirled to share her excitement with Jess, but her brother was standing solemnly in the doorway.

"I wouldn't gamble on it," he said. "Dad checked the records. Stampede has had six colts, but she's never had a filly." He lead the horse inside.

That night Cassie tried sneaking to bed ahead of Patsy. She knew what her sister would say about the time she had picked to ask. She'd say it was as dumb as acting like a frog and climbing the hallway walls as Cassie had when she was little. Cassie didn't want to discuss it with anybody. She was exhausted from the ordeal as it was. But before the door was even closed, Patsy barged in and plopped on the bed.

"Talk about a dumb time to ask," she said. "Why did you do a thing like that?"

"Because I'm dumb," Cassie said. She jumped in bed, pulled the covers over her head and wouldn't listen to another word.

Even though it was Saturday, Cassie woke early the following morning. Birds were singing outside her window, and the day looked bright and beckoning, the kind that says, "Get up, today's the day." But Cassie flopped back on the pillow. Her chance was over. She stayed in bed as long as she could.

Even when Cassie did get up, she tried hard to blend in with the surroundings. She tried not to be alone with Patsy or to remember last night's blunder. But she didn't have to suffer all day. Right after lunch Celine came pounding up the driveway on Thunder. Her brown riding boots exactly matched the color of her blouse, and a pink scarf held the blond curls flying behind her.

"Guess what?" she yelled, jumping from the saddle at the steps.

"What?" Patsy begged.

Cassie still wasn't anxious for company, especially not Celine's. She didn't want her to ask about dad's answer, so she tried to look excited about her friend's news too. "What?" she asked.

Celine didn't even take time to catch her breath. "Mother and I were at the new mall. The grand opening is two weeks from today, and they're having a drawing." She looked deliberately from Cassie to Patsy and back again. "The top prize is a horse."

A horse! That did excite Cassie.

''Of course, you have to be eighteen to register,'' Celine went on, ''or have someone with you who is. I registered. I was with mother.'' By now Cassie's mind was racing. Jess, of course, she could get Jess. He'd go with her to register.

''I saw a picture of the one they're giving.'' Celine leaned forward. ''Did you ask your dad?''

''What does it look like?'' Cassie asked quickly. ''The horse they're giving, I mean. Tell me all about it.'' She pretended not to hear the question.

Celine shrugged a little. ''Oh, you know, brown, four legs.'' She shot a glance at her mare, whipped the scarf from her curls and shook them loose. ''Of course it can't begin to compare with Thunder, but still and all. . . . Oh, Cass,'' she sighed, ''can't you do *something* with your hair?''

That irked the daylights out of Cassie. Here they were in the middle of discussing a horse, and Celine pulls her ''look at beautiful me'' act. It almost made her ill, and she nearly said so, but then she changed her mind. Celine had let her know about the drawing. ''I just got up,'' she said.

Celine jumped back in the saddle. ''Well, I wanted to let you know. Riding together *might* be fun.''

As soon as their friend was out of sight, Patsy grabbed Cassie by the arm. ''What do you think, Cassie?'' Should we register?''

Cassie was way ahead. 'Of course,'' she said. ''Why would we pass up a chance like that? There's nothing to lose. I'll get Jess to take us.''

The rest of the day went faster. Patsy didn't say anything more about last evening, and Cassie spent the time speculating about the horse and waiting for a chance to speak with Jess alone. It didn't come 'til evening when he took the horses to the barn. She waited by the basswood tree until he finished, and then hurried up the drive to meet him.

"Jess," she said, "I have a favor to ask."

"Fire away," he said, and hopped the shallow ditch to lean against the rail fence. Cassie jumped the ditch too.

"They're having a drawing for prizes at the new mall. I want to register, but you have to be eighteen or have someone with you who is. It's so there's a chance you'll buy something, I guess. Will you take me?" She hopped on the rail beside him. "First prize is a horse."

"A riding horse?"

Cassie nodded, and Jess strung a long thin whistle through his teeth. "Nice prize. Think I'll register myself."

"Oh, Jess, what would you do with a horse?"

"Take care of it." That was true. There was *no* animal Jess wouldn't take care of.

"But I want to ride it."

"I'm just teasing," he said, "but I doubt the 18-year-old requirement is so you'll buy something."

"What else would it be for?"

"More likely," Jess said, "adult approval. So if you won, they'd know it was all right with your parents that you keep the horse."

Cassie straightened up on the rail. "Well, if I won it, it wouldn't cost anything. It'd be free."

"Initially, yes," Jess agreed, "but not on the long run. It costs to keep anything."

Cassie swallowed. ''You mean . . . you mean you think dad wouldn't let me keep the horse?''

Jess held up his hand. ''I didn't say that, but I was thinking of what he said.'' Cassie remembered dad's words too, *We don't need one more thing that can't pay its way.*

''Could the horse skid logs?'' she asked.

''Not a riding horse.''

''It wouldn't cost *much* to keep, would it? Maybe I could get a job.''

''You're too young for a job,'' Jess said. He thought a minute more, then swung around and pulled her hair. ''Aw, forget it. With five thousand names in that bucket, the odds will be pretty slim anyway. Sure, I'll take you.''

''Thanks,'' Cassie said, ''thanks a lot.'' She skipped to the house and threw all the complications to the wind. If she won that horse, mother would help. So would Jess. She'd find some way to keep him.

Early the next week Jess took Cassie to register. They went in his truck, and Patsy went too, because two names were better than one.

Cassie spotted the picture of the horse as soon as they entered the mall. She hurried toward it. Oh, it was a handsome mare, more black than brown, and glistening as every cared-for horse should. It's back was straight and strong, and it had long legs and small pointed ears that stood at attention. It didn't have a red mane, and she couldn't get a real good look at the eyes; the photo wasn't that clear. Yet if the horse lacked anything she might have requested by choice, owning it would more than compensate. Her hand was shaking as she wrote her name and phone number. She whispered a prayer as she dropped it in the box, "Please, God, let it be mine."

Once the paper was in the box, Cassie forgot all the ifs, and the horse became a reality. Her horse. She could imagine she was riding, the insides of her thighs pressed against the great warm body, her knees hugging its ribs and her cheek dusted by a touch of the mane as she crouched toward its neck.

She began thinking of names. Star was her favorite, but it couldn't be that because this horse didn't have a star. Misty was special too, but that didn't fit the color. How about Beauty, Midnight, or Velvet? Or were they too common? Maybe Silk would be better. But she knew naming wouldn't be any real problem. She had a notebook filled with names.

"Do you think we'll win?" Patsy asked as they got back in the truck.

Cassie was still going over names. She sighed a long sigh and let the picture of the prize horse fix in a deep, firm place in her mind. "If praying and wishing count for anything," she said, "I'm sure."

5
Some People Have All the Luck

The following week Cassie thought of nothing but the horse. Every morning and every night she prayed for it to be hers. Not only that, she whispered a prayer every time the thought crossed her mind, which was most of the time. She found it difficult to sit still in the classroom or to concentrate on her schoolwork. One day in class she was daydreaming about the horse as usual when she heard her name being repeated somewhere off in the distance. When she suddenly realized it wasn't in the distance and jerked to answer, the whole class was snickering, all except Mrs. Milford who looked quite stern.

''Cassie,'' she said, ''you must keep your mind on your work if you intend to make it through exams.'' Cassie felt the heat rising from her neck to her face.

''Oh, I do,'' she said. ''My thoughts wandered for just a minute.''

''That's strange,'' Mrs. Milford said. ''The whole class has been watching you for five.''

Everyone snickered again, all except Patsy. She had her head buried in her book. Cassie buried her head too, but she could still hear the others.

''All right, class,'' Mrs. Milford said finally, ''everyone back to work. Now what was the date of the Louisiana Purchase?''

The Louisiana Purchase, Cassie thought. All this suspense tearing at her insides, and she was supposed to concentrate on the Louisiana Purchase. What bearing could that possibly have on the present? She glanced over at Patsy and immediately thought of one reason. If she didn't pass the exams, she'd heard only a rumble of the thunder to come, and that wouldn't help anything. So she tried to buckle down to the work. Still it was the longest week she'd ever spent.

On Friday, at dismissal time, Celine came to sit with Cassie and Patsy on the bus.

''Are you going to town for the drawing tomorrow?'' she asked.

Cassie didn't answer. Neither she nor Patsy had told anyone but Jess about it. She looked at her sister.

''Of course, you don't have to be there to win, but it's such fun to be part of the excitement.'' Celine pretended to shiver all over. "Mother's taking me."

"I . . . I don't know," Patsy began. "Mother doesn't. . . ."

"Mother may have other plans," Cassie said.

Celine lifted one eyebrow. "We could stop for you, I suppose. I'm sure *my* mother wouldn't mind. Shall we plan on it then?"

"I'll call you in the morning," Cassie said. After Celine left the bus, Patsy turned toward her.

"You don't suppose Jess would take us?"

Cassie shook her head. "Not a chance. He couldn't get away for a minute. You know what mother says about planting. Dad can't even sleep 'til that's out of the way."

Patsy nodded. "And after that it's worrying about rain. Should we ask mother, go with Celine, or stay home?" She squirmed in the seat and answered part of her own question. "I'm sure Celine would call us as soon as she knew, but I'm not sure I want to hear the news from her, especially if it's bad."

"And if it's good," Cassie said, "she's bound to make it sound like she's giving the horse. I'd prefer asking mother."

Patsy agreed. "You'll ask?"

"I'll ask," Cassie said. She decided to do it at dishwashing time. First she would tell mother they had registered. She could count on her to understand.

But while they were eating, mother announced plans of her own. "If the car is free tomorrow," she said to dad, "I'd like to use it to go to town. The garden plot is ready, but I don't have seeds. I need cleaning supplies too.'

"That's all right with me," dad said. "Jess and I will be busy 'til late with the grain."

Mother turned to the girls. "Would you care to go along? You'd have to finish your Saturday chores first."

"I would," Patsy said.

"Me too," Cassie echoed. "I'll get up real early."

In the morning Cassie got up without being called and woke Patsy. They cleaned their room, folded clothes as they came from the dryer, and did the porches. At about eleven o'clock mother called them to get ready and Cassie hurried to her room to change. She could hardly get into her clean things fast enough, but she did take time to brush her hair in case they took a picture.

"Patsy and I would like to go to the new mall," Cassie said to mother on the way. "They're having a grand opening today. Lots of prizes and stuff."

"That sounds like fun," mother said. "I have some errands there too." Cassie could hardly believe it. Everything was going their way. If only it lasted until the drawing for the horse. Her hand began trembling on the arm rest.

At the mall the parking lot was filled with cars. Cassie could hardly hold herself to a walk as they went inside. A large crowd had already gathered around the center fountain.

"That's where they're drawing names for the prizes," Cassie said. "Let's go there."

"You girls go ahead," mother said. "I'll do my shopping and we'll meet later. How about the dime store in 45 minutes?"

''Thanks, mom,'' Cassie said. ''We'll meet you there.'' Grabbing Patsy by the arm she wormed her way through the crowd until they were quite near the fountain where there was a small stage.

''Shall we look for Celine?'' Patsy whispered.

''No,'' Cassie said. It would be too painful to hear her if they lost. ''Squeeze this way so you can see.''

They didn't have to wait long. Soon some men in suits gathered around the stage. When things were organized, the mayor was the first to be introduced. He gave a little speech. Then a girl with a glittery crown cut a ribbon. She was a Miss Somebody or Other—Cassie wasn't listening and couldn't remember. Then they brought out the lesser prizes: a toaster, a blanket, lawn chairs, a picnic table—the drawing began. An older man won the toaster. A lady in a green coat got the blanket. Two other names were drawn. There were squeals and smiles and ''Thank you's,'' but Cassie couldn't keep track any more. Her mind was on one thing alone. Finally, from the hall behind, came the echoed sound of sharp, clacking steps. They were bringing in the horse.

Cassie whirled to look. On tiptoes she saw a beautiful black head. There were squeals and sighs of delight. Someone stepped on her toes. Then the horse passed where she stood, and the warm odor of large animal met her nostrils. The trembling began again. ''Please, God, please,'' she begged.

It seemed that the man shook the box forever. Finally he held it high and asked another to pull the name.

''The winner of the grand prize—this beautiful black mare is . . .!'' He opened the paper, and Cassie's heart stood still.

''It goes to a young lady,'' he called loudly. ''Celine Finette!''

Celine! The name hung in the air like a great suffocating ball, and the lump in Cassie's chest rose to meet it. Celine who already had a horse! There was a shriek, and Celine rushed forward.

''I can't believe it!'' she squealed. She was jumping, hopping, and bouncing all at the same time. ''I've never won anything before. Are you sure? Oh, I just can't believe it!''

Cassie couldn't believe it either. A great numbing wound inside made it almost impossible to keep back the tears. Life wasn't fair. She turned to leave, but someone stepped in front of her. Looking up, her eyes met Celine's. There was a long moment, then Cassie swallowed and held out her hand. ''She . . . she's very beautiful,'' she said.

Celine grabbed Cassie. She threw her arms around Patsy too, and jumped again. ''Oh, I'm so excited. I think I'm going to blow right up. You have to ride home with me and keep me from exploding all over the car. You just *have* to!'' it sounded so artificial, yet Cassie couldn't let anyone know how she felt.

''I'll ride with you,'' she said. ''Patsy, will you meet mother?''

Patsy nodded and went, and Cassie was left with Celine who was still jumping all over. They took pictures. Flashbulbs popped. Celine smiled, posed, and held her face close to the horse, but Cassie was on the outside, and it was pure pain. The ride home seemed to take forever, too, especially with Celine carrying on all the way. Yet, no matter how it hurt, and it did, Cassie knew she couldn't blame her friend. It was only a game of chance.

Finally Celine's mother let Cassie off at the drive. She held up her hand in goodby, then turned and started toward the basswood tree. She was going to climb it because she wanted to be alone, but dad had the truck parked near it so she went to the house instead. Mother was in the kitchen fixing supper and Cassie sat at the table.

"Why do some people have all the luck?" she asked.

Mother stopped stirring. "About the horse, you mean? Patsy told me. I wonder," she went on, "if Celine thinks she's as lucky as you think she is."

"Of course she does," Cassie said. "You should hear her."

Mother dried her hands and came to the table. "But what can she really do with two horses?"

"Ride them," Cassie said.

"I suppose she could," mother said, "if that's what she really wants, but she's had one horse all along, and she hasn't been satisfied just to ride that."

"I think she has," Cassie said.

"Then why is she here all the time?" mother asked, "or over at Mary's?"

"She wants to show off?" Cassie didn't like to say it.

Mother shook her head. "I think Celine wants something you already have, someone to be with, a friend. You have one day and night, and brothers, and a dad who cares about you enough to always be here."

Celine's dad was never home. He worked away. Cassie hadn't ever thought much about it.

''But the way she brags. . . .''

''Maybe she has to,'' mother said, ''to keep you from knowing how she really feels.'' Cassie felt a twinge at that. She still hadn't told Celine that dad had said no.

''But why would she be lonely? She has everything.''

Just then the front door slammed and Patsy came racing in. ''Cassie, look,'' she cried, pointing to the window. ''Here comes Celine, and she's bringing the horse.''

6
Ramona

Cassie ran to the doorway. Sure enough, Celine was riding Thunder and leading the new horse behind. She turned in at the driveway, and Cassie got herself ready.

"They didn't waste any time delivering her," she said when Celine was close enough to hear.

"They had the trailer all ready. Someone want to take a quick ride?"

"Sure," Cassie said. "Will it be all right if we both go?"

"I guess, but you'll both have to ride Ramona. She's thicker than Thunder."

"Ramona," Cassie repeated. "Is that what you've named her?"

Celine tossed her curls a little. "It's foreign and sophisticated sounding, like some of the places my father goes. I already called dad about him. Well, let's go."

"I'll handle the reins," Cassie said. She put a bare foot in the stirrup, flung her other leg over Ramona's back and met the saddle. Ramona took a small step sideways. She didn't feel thick at all, but alive and warm and wonderful. A tingle rippled through Cassie just under the skin. She tried not to smile too much. Patsy got on behind her.

"We'll go north," Celine said, "but stay behind me. Thunder is sensitive, and I don't want her to think she's second fiddle."

Right then Cassie would have been satisfied to stay behind anybody. She made the clicking sound she had practiced for months. Ramona moved beneath her, and they fell in line behind Celine and Thunder. Patsy held tightly onto Cassie's waist, but Cassie sat up straight and tall. The saddle was smooth and firm against her legs, and one hand rested casually on the horn. That one held the reins. With the other she touched Ramona's dark sleek coat. It was smooth as silk, and Cassie felt almost like a queen.

Cassie didn't even think of passing Celine. The music of Ramona's hooves clacking against the blacktop road was enough to satisfy her for the moment. They started to trot. Ramona's head rose and fell to a springy, perky beat. It was a little bouncy, but Cassie didn't mind at all.

At the recreational trail Celine turned Thunder left. The trail circled around the old county swamp and met the blacktop again further up the line.

"It's fun to gallop," Celine called. "Shall we try?"

"Go ahead," Cassie called, "we're right behind you." She felt Patsy tighten her grip.

Celine leaned forward and Thunder moved on. Cassie leaned forward too. For just a second Ramona's step felt choppy. Then she stretched her long legs to the wind, and it was like heaven, as if she were riding the large swelling waves of the sea, soaring up to the crest and falling gently into the trough again. With her hair blowing in the wind and Ramona's mane billowing before her, she was riding the melody of a flowing perfect rhythm. It was glory. Cassie wished it could go on forever.

But soon Celine pulled Thunder in. Cassie hated to, but she checked Ramona too. She broke her stride, slowed further, and then came to a stop. Celine turned her horse around.

"We won't go further," she said. "Thunder can take it, but I don't believe Ramona is as well bred. Besides, she was carrying both of you." She smoothed the curls on her shoulders. "Still I did need someone to give her a try." Cassie didn't say anything. She followed Celine back to the house and stopped at the porch.

"I'll rub her down." Cassie said as she slid from the saddle. The horse wasn't really sweating.

"Bart will do that when I get home," Celine said. "That's why we hired him."

"All right," Cassie said, but she knew that if Ramona were hers, Bart wouldn't be needed. She'd do it herself. Her hand went to Ramona's jaw, and she brought her face close to the horse's. This time Cassie could see her eyes clearly. They looked right into hers. "Thanks for the ride," she whispered. "It was heaven."

"Look out for your toes," Celine chirped from her perch. Cassie glanced down at her bare feet right next to Ramona's hooves. Celine wore boots, and Patsy had shoes.

"I'm not worried," she said. "Ramona knows my feet from the ground."

Celine shrugged and glanced at Patsy. "I've had a horse longer than she has."

"Thanks again," Cassie said and handed over the reins.

Celine left, leading Ramona behind her, and the girls went inside. It was supper time, and everyone was already at the table. Cassie slid into her chair without even washing her hands. She didn't want to destroy the gentle horse odor. Dad said grace and Cassie heard him mention needed rain, but she didn't pay special attention to his words. She whispered her own, "Thank you, thank you, thank you." Ramona wasn't hers, but someday. . . . She was still thinking of the ride when mother's voice caught her attention.

"Cassie, will you pour dad's coffee?"

"Of course," she said, and did it without really thinking. She didn't want to think of anything else, only the ride and the horse.

"How was the ride?" mother asked a little later.

"Wonderful," Cassie said softly, "just wonderful."

For once the dishes were done in a hurry. As soon as they were finished, Cassie slipped to the basswood tree. Patsy didn't like curling her fingers and toes into that big, black hole. She was afraid a squirrel might nip her fingers. Nor did she think the trunk was sturdy enough. Cassie knew better, but Patsy was free to think what she would. Anyway, Cassie liked having the tree to herself. Ducking below the low-hanging branches, Cassie curled her toes around the wound in the old leaning trunk, and ran all the way up to the first branches. A few swings and she was another fifteen feet above them. There, nestled into a comfortable crotch, she let the rustling breeze carry her away and she was riding Ramona once more.

She felt the ride all over again, Ramona's legs reaching to the wind, curling beneath her muscled shoulders for power, and grabbing the wind another time. Her mane lifted, tail stretched out long and low behind, and Cassie was part of it all. That's why she liked the old tree. In it she could be anywhere she wanted. Nothing was unattainable, no place was distant, nothing impossible. All of it was hers, the whole wide world. And right now she was soaring on Ramona. Or a horse very much like her. She realized it couldn't be Ramona, because the horse had a coat warm as cinnamon with a red mane.

7
Who's Going to Arizona?

Cassie stayed in the tree a long time. The sky was darkening when at last she saw Jess come to the corral to take the horses inside. She watched her brother stroke Lightning's long head and scratch behind his ears, and she heard the promise of feed when he was inside. Then he came for Stampede. He coaxed her gently, chided softly when she threatened to prance in the other direction, and coaxed again.

"It's clouding up, girl," he said, "and spring rains are chilly. No good for you or your foal." He went back to the barn for feed. Finally he caught the halter, and led Stampede in. That Jess, he had a way with everything. He was on his way down the drive when the front door of the house slammed, and mother and Patsy stepped onto the porch.

"She disappeared right after the dishes were done," Cassie heard her sister say. "I don't know where she is."

Mother cupped her hands around her mouth. "Cassie," she called, "where are you?" Cassie hated to answer, not because she wanted to make trouble, or for any particular reason, but only because answering would change things. She waited a minute. Then she heard Jess.

"I'll get her," he called.

"All right," mother said. She opened the door and she and Patsy went back inside. Cassie relaxed again. It wasn't that she minded going in or even having mother know she was in the tree. She just wanted to be alone, to do things in her own time. She didn't want to be crowded.

Jess didn't crowd her. Cassie was sure he knew where she was, yet he didn't rush right over. Instead he sauntered into the corral, kicked out some thistles that were springing up, and flung some small rocks in the ditch. Hanging both arms over the rail, he stood a while listening to the frog chorus in the cranberry swamp croaking their nightly spring tunes. Finally he sauntered over to the tree, broke off a dead twig and snapped it into pieces. It was almost dark, but Cassie could still see him.

"Doing anything special?" he asked at last.

."Doing nothing," Cassie said. She broke a twig and snapped it too.

"Well," he said, "sometimes nothing can take a long time."

"Come on up," she said.

Her brother seemed neither surprised nor insulted by her invitation. He curled his fingers around the wound and walked up the trunk just the way she did. It made Cassie smile a little. He was so different from Patsy. When he reached the first branch, Jess stretched his long legs to the younger part, swung over, and found a place to sit. The branches were sturdy but not too thick. He looked east and west and every other way there was to look. Then he did it all over again.

''You come here often?'' he asked.

''Sometimes,'' Cassie said, ''when I have to be free.'' She wasn't sure what she expected him to say.

Jess didn't say anything, not at first, but in a little while he answered. ''I know. The rope does tighten.''

''For you too?''

He grinned a little. ''Especially when dad starts in about the forty.''

Cassie smiled too. ''But you *will* buy it.''

''I don't know,'' Jess said slowly. He looked off in the distance where everything on the horizon was silhouetted against the western sky. ''I'd like to see the rest of the country.''

''The rest of the country?'' Cassie asked. ''What for?''

Her brother shrugged. ''I don't know. Sometimes I just feel caged up. I'd like to hike in the mountains, travel the rivers, tramp the desert. I just want to see.'' He sounded so different.

''Then why don't you go?'' Cassie said.

''It's not that simple.'' Her brother snapped another twig. ''I'd hate to turn on dad.''

''But you wouldn't be turning on him.'' Jess had

always been the one dad could count on.

"He'd think so."

"But you'd be back."

"I don't know." Don't know? Of course, he'd be back. Jess loved the place. He loved the fields, the woods, the animals, even the tree he was in. Look how he took care of the calves and Lightning. Why, he could even train Stampede if dad would let him. Cassie knew he'd be back, but her brother sounded so uncertain she didn't say so.

"It's just that . . . well," he went on, "if I buy the forty, it has to be my decision, and if I don't go, how will I ever know?"

Cassie let that sink in for a minute. "Then," she said, "you'll have to go."

"We'll see," Jess said. "Right now I wish those clouds would gather up and bring in some rain. It would sprout the seeds and take some worry off dad too." He unwound his legs and dropped to the ground.

Cassie slid from the tree too and, following her brother to the house, she studied his broad shoulders and the strong curve of his lightly bearded jaw which she could see when he turned his head to the side. So Jess had his dreams too. But he still looked sturdy as a rock. Cassie thought about it a long time that night.

Sunday afternoon was long. It always was when Cassie was thinking about the horse she didn't have, and the ride of yesterday had only intensified her longing. Though she and Celine had their differences, Cassie sat by the window hoping she might come over with Ramona. She waited a long time. At last she did see Celine, and the horses were with her. Cassie straightened up in the sofa, but Celine didn't turn in at their drive. She went right on by, to Mary's, Cassie thought. She slumped back on the sofa again. Well, she couldn't plan on Ramona, and even if there was an occasional ride, it still wasn't the same as having her own horse. She was glad when it began to drizzle a little, but it still didn't shorten the day.

By evening the drizzle had stopped, but the dampness kept Cassie inside. She reached to the bottom of her bureau drawer and pulled out the *Scholastic* magazine she had saved since third grade. It told all about a government program called Adopt a Horse. She walked to the kitchen where mother was writing out the week's menu. Patsy was there too. She was reading a book and fingering the curls she had done that morning. They looked just like Celine's did yesterday. Jess had taken a cookie from the jar and was leaning against the counter eating. Dad was in the other room watching tv.

Cassie sat down, flattened the paper on the table, and tucked her hanging hair behind one ear. She took a deep breath and slowly and deliberately read aloud from the front page exactly as she had done so many times before. "The wild horses of the West have always had to run for their lives. Now they are in trouble again. See page 2." Ceremoniously she turned the cover.

Mother stopped writing. "Cassie," she said patiently, "we've been through that before."

Cassie smoothed the second page. It wasn't mother's reaction she was looking for. Mostly she wanted Jess to hear. ''High in the dry Arizona countryside. . . .'' she began again, but Patsy reached over and covered the page with her book.

''That paper is a hundred years old,'' she said.

''It is not,'' Cassie said. ''It's four.''

''It might as well be.''

''Why?''

''Because there's no way we can travel the hundreds of miles out West to bring back a horse.'' Patsy stuck her face forward and flipped her curls exactly the way Celine did. ''Nobody here is going to Arizona.''

It made Cassie's blood boil to see her sister imitate Celine like that, especially when she knew how badly Celine's act bugged Cassie. And maybe one ride on Ramona was enough to satisfy her sister, but it wasn't enough to satisfy Cassie. She poked her face back. ''Jess is,'' she said. ''He can bring it back.''

Patsy's mouth fell open. Mother turned around in her chair. For just a moment Cassie felt like king of the hill, but then she looked at Jess. With the cookie half way to his mouth, he stood staring straight ahead. Dad was in the doorway.

''Who's going to Arizona?'' he asked.

8
A Little Bit of Patience

Cassie couldn't say anything. The newspaper was at dad's side, and he took his glasses from his face. Patsy was the one to answer.

"Jess is," she said. "Cassie said so."

A big knot rose in Cassie's chest. For once she wanted to be like Celine, smooth it over, say things like, "Some day, on vacation, maybe," but it wouldn't come out. "He . . . he didn't really say Arizona," she blurted. "He said mountains, desert. . . ." Her voice trailed off. It sounded so phony.

"Traveling takes money," dad said.

Cassie jumped in again. "Oh, he's got the money. He's got. . . ." And then she wished she could melt right into the floor. It was the money for the forty.

A strange stiff look came to dad's face. He was almost

white. "So you don't want to buy it," he said. "You're willing to throw all this over, everything I've worked for."

"Dad, I. . . ." Jess looked pale too. Cassie knew he was trying to choose words, but his voice hung in mid-air, and dad didn't wait.

"That forty would make this farm the most valuable around. Another ten years and it would all be yours. Yet you're willing to leave it all, walk off and. . . ."

"Dad," Jess pleaded, "it's not that way."

"That's the way it looks from here," dad said. He whirled and walked from the doorway.

Cassie ran to her brother. It was as bad as the time she'd picked to ask for the horse, as bad as the times she'd run up the walls of the hallway. "Oh, Jess," she cried, "I didn't mean to tell, I. . . ."

"It's all right," her brother said. He didn't even look angry. "It had to come out sometime."

Sometime, yes, Cassie thought, but not now. Not from her mouth. Why did she always do those things? There was nothing more she could say so she turned to run from the room. She wanted to go the tree, but it was still too wet out, so she ran to her room instead and plopped on the bed. It seemed that she'd wanted a horse forever. She'd hoped and prayed. She'd asked God and her dad, and it really didn't seem that either one was listening. Or maybe they just didn't understand. She was trying to be a decent kid. She was trying not to grow up too fast or stay little too long. She was trying to do what she was supposed to do, but it wasn't working. If only she had something of her own, something to count on, to understand. As always that need was answered by a horse.

Cassie punched her pillow a few times and propped it under her head. She even tried punching the horse out of her mind, but the picture kept coming back, a soft, silken nose for tenderness, deep patient eyes gazing into hers, someone to walk if she wanted to walk, or rest if she wanted to rest. Someone to let her be herself. It would save her from doing all the dumb things she was tempted to do again. But how could she ever get that horse? She couldn't ask dad again. If only God would listen, but he seemed so far away.

In the morning Cassie went to mother. She was in the kitchen and closer. "Why can't we have a horse?" she asked again. "I've prayed and prayed, and I don't think God even hears."

Mother was beating eggs. "I wouldn't be so sure about that," she said. "Did you ever ask him to help you do the right things so that a horse might be yours?"

"The right things?" Cassie said. "Like what?"

"Like being patient," mother said. "By recognizing all dad has done for you already, by respecting that his burdens are larger than yours." She stopped beating and looked straight into Cassie's eyes. "He's responsible for the whole family, you know."

Cassie did know. "But I've been patient," she said. "I've waited two years already. Isn't that enough?"

"I don't know," mother said. "I've never had a schedule to follow. I do know that God is very patient with us."

"And it's hard," Cassie insisted. "I think about having a horse all the time, like Patsy thinks about growing up. She worries about it."

Mother smiled a little. ''Patsy will grow up whether she worries about it or not, and a bit of patience makes the waiting much more pleasant. Lots of things are like that, Cassie.'' She started beating again. Right then Patsy came into the kitchen, and that ended the conversation. It didn't seem like much of an answer to Cassie, at least not then.

Later, when she had a chance to think about it, it did make some sense, especially the part about growing up. Cassie remembered when she could hardly see above the kitchen counter. Now both she and Patsy could easily reach the first cupboard above it. They'd grown that much, and she, at least, hadn't done any worrying about it. She doubted Patsy had either, to that point. Patience might work with the growing up part, but she still didn't see how it could help with getting a horse. That looked like a long way off.

The rain that was needed didn't come that week. Dad mentioned it constantly, and Cassie knew it was on her brother's mind too. He kept watching the sky. The things she had brought up seemed to be on everyone's mind too. At least it was uncomfortably quiet around the place. Oh, they talked about rain and planting, and repairing, and a few other things, but no one said anything about the things that really mattered, like Arizona, the forty, or a horse. Cassie was getting so itchy. Horses were all Celine and Mary talked about.

By Thursday the air at the dinner table was as heavy as bricks. Under the table Cassie scraped her bare feet together to release some of the pressure, but it didn't help much. Finally she excused herself before she suffocated and started down the hallway, and suddenly, she couldn't stand it a minute longer. She had to have a horse or blow into a million pieces. In one thrust she threw herself upward, clamped her bare feet and hands onto both walls and ran right to the ceiling, just like she did when she was little. If she looked like a frog, Cassie didn't mind. If she *was* a frog, she didn't care. At least she was doing something besides waiting.

Right then Patsy came to the hallway and stopped in her tracks, "Mother," she screeched, "Cassie's doing it again."

Cassie dropped to the floor only a moment before mother figured out what the "it" was and appeared at the doorway. Cassie ducked into her room so she didn't have to say anything. Saying didn't do any good anyway.

The next morning at breakfast mother made an announcement. "The crops are all planted," she said, "and it's been lots of work. The last weeks of school are not fun either. Everyone's nerves are on edge. We do need rain, but no amount of worry and tension will help that. Dad and I, with patience, are leaving that matter in the hands of the good Lord and are going away for the weekend. Jess will take care of the chores, and we'll all have a couple days away from each other. Maybe that will help too." She looked quite hopeful.

Dad didn't look nearly as confident. He didn't say anything, but for once he was letting mother take the reins. Cassie was glad for that. She didn't know how they could last the whole weekend without a full scale explosion anyway.

In bed that night Cassie thought about her problem once more. She couldn't ask dad for a horse again. Patsy was no help, and mother's answer was words. Jess was the only one who seemed to care at all. In the morning as soon as mother and dad had left, she went to the barn where he was working.

"There's only one chance of me ever getting a horse," she said. "That's if Stampede settles down so dad can sell her as a trained mare and get his money back."

"I think you're right."

Cassie looked her brother straight in the eye. "And you can train her. I know that."

He agreed again. "But dad won't let me."

"Dad's not here," Cassie said.

"He's only gone for the weekend. It'll take more time than that."

Cassie shook her head. "I've got an idea. We'll fix up a load she can't prance away with. She'll have to slow down. Then you can begin to reason with her."

Her brother didn't look convinced. "I don't think so, Cassie. I don't think you can force any living thing into your way. I think. . . ."

Cassie broke right in. "We'll use the big, old, tractor tire behind the shed, put some boards in the middle and heap it with the sandbags we used when the bridge threatened to go out."

"It isn't something that can be done like that,

Cassie. We have to wait until. . . ." But Cassie refused to let him finish.

"If dad can get his money back," she said, "*he* can make the down payment on the forty."

Jess hesitated for only another moment. "You win," he said. "We'll give it one try."

9 Quite a Surprise

Cassie ran for the shed. The huge tire was still there and would account for a lot of weight itself. A logging chain was wrapped around it from the time dad had used it to drag a trail. Next she found two wide boards to make a bottom. A pry pole helped her place them. Then came the real work. She dragged the sand bags, 22 of them, one corner at a time until she had them loaded. They weighed about 50 pounds apiece. That would slow Stampede down. In fact, Cassie wasn't sure she could pull it at all. She knew she herself couldn't move one more bag. Her arms felt like jelly. She plopped on the load to rest.

"Let's see," she figured. "Fifty times 22 makes 1100 pounds. And the tire must weigh at least 100. That ought to do the trick."

Before long she heard the north door open, and Jess came out leading Stampede. The big mare followed without incident until they came to the corral gate where she was accustomed to turning in. As soon as they passed it she tossed her head and nickered loudly.

"It's OK, girl," Jess said. "Nobody is going to hurt you. We're only going to try the harness."

The words didn't soothe the Belgian at all. Her legs stiffened, and she went into that crazy, unnatural prance that resembled a stiff-legged bounce. Her head tossed nervously.

"It's all right," Jess said soothingly to the horse. Then he said quietly to Cassie, "It would be better to only lead her around, give her a little more time. I don't think we can force her our way."

"But we don't have more time," Cassie insisted. "Dad will be back tomorrow night and put a stop to the whole thing, and neither of us will be one bit ahead of where we are right now."

"OK," Jess said. "One try." He tied Stampede to the post. "Help me get the harness."

It was a full regalia of straps, buckles, collar, and reins—heavy. Cassie never could have lifted it alone or figured out how it went, let alone put it on.

"Whoa, girl," Jess said as he hoisted the contraption above the horse. It plopped on her back. Stampede backed sharply and tested the rope. She swung her hindquarters from one side to the other and her feet thudded against the hard, dry ground, whooshing the long hair at her hooves. Cassie moved back. Bare feet were no match for those huge hooves.

"I don't know . . ." Jess began again.

"The weight will do it," Cassie said. She tugged one more sand bag onto the load. "That makes 1250 pounds. She won't prance off with that."

Jess didn't look so sure. He fit the harness straps all around and hooked them securely. Finally he hooked the chain to the singletree, untied the halter rope from the post, and taking the reins firmly in both hands, set his feet on the sand bags. "OK," he said to Cassie, "stay out of the way." He clicked a signal to Stampede.

But Cassie had no intention of staying behind. She leaped to the bags and grabbed her brother's belt just as Stampede hit the load. Her head snapped backward, and she was nearly jolted loose. There wasn't time for Jess to object.

"Hang on," he yelled.

Cassie grabbed his belt with her other hand. She couldn't believe it. The whole load was being yanked across the ground in wild, leaping jerks.

"Whoa!" Jess yelled. "Whoa!" He leaned back pulling on the reins, but Stampede wouldn't stop.

"When we hit the gravel, she'll stop," Cassie yelled. They did, and it didn't slow them a bit. Jess had no control. Stampede's head was tilted forward, her muscles bulged with power. She was hitting on all fours, and the load leaped along behind. She headed straight for the barn and the old stone milkhouse.

Cassie was struck with panic. If they weren't going to crash into a building, they would have to make a sharp curve to the narrow drive between the two. Could they do it? Ahead she saw Patsy standing aghast with her hands covering her mouth.

Stampede whipped around the corner. The tire hit

the drive, and choking dust flew up around them. All Cassie could think of was a chariot race to the death in the days of the Roman empire. Through the dust the stone building came toward her.

The load didn't clear. It clipped the corner of the milkhouse, and Cassie lost her grip on Jess's belt. She flew from the bags. Something slammed her legs, and she hit the gravel, choking and pawing at the dust. She couldn't see anything. Then suddenly Patsy was at her side.

"Are you dead? Are you dead?" her sister kept yelling.

Cassie tried to sit up, feeling somewhere between numb and hurting all over. She looked at her legs. They were there, but covered with blood and dirt. The numbness began to recede and the general pain started to localize on parts of her body. Her shoulder hurt, and her entire arm. Patsy was crying out loud. Then Cassie thought of Jess. What had happened to him? She managed to raise herself partway and saw him through the settling dust. Stampede had crossed the blacktop road and was headed across the field. Jess was still on the load, yanking desperately on the reins.

"Stop," Cassie yelled. "Stop, you beast." Then she realized she was crying too, and she couldn't do anything to help. She could only sit and watch.

Finally Stampede stopped. Jess unhooked the chain, took the halter rope and hurried toward home, leading a skittish Stampede.

With Patsy helping, Cassie got to her feet. Her whole right side—leg, shoulder, and hip—stung unmercifully. Her shirt and shorts were shredded, but she limped to meet Jess.

Stampede was wet with sweat. Her eyes were still wild, and her nostrils flaring. Jess tied her at the corral and came running.

"Thank God you're alive," he said. "Are you badly hurt? Did you hit the building?"

"I couldn't see what happened," Patsy said. "She was lost in the dust."

Cassie held out a hand toward him. "I don't think I did. I think it's just gravel burns."

"Thank God," her brother said again. "I was afraid you were killed, or lost a leg or a foot. If they were caught between. . . ." He quit talking, scooped her up in his arms, and took her to the house. There he looked at her limbs and shoulder carefully. They were terribly scraped. "Do you think you need to go to the hospital?" he asked.

"I don't think so," Cassie said. "I think mother would make me soak the dirt out."

"I'll help you," Patsy said. She started running water in the tub.

Jess helped Cassie to the bathroom. "OK," he said, "I'll take care of things outside and come back."

He left and Patsy helped Cassie into the tub. The stinging was worse when she hit the water. The pain became fierce. It brought out beads of perspiration on her forehead, and her stomach felt sick. She wanted to get out.

"I'll cool it a little," Patsy said. "Maybe that will help." She added a little mild soap too.

The cooler temperature did help a little. Cassie steeled herself and got all the wounds under water. She stayed in the tub as long as she could stand it. When she got out, the scrapes looked better even though they didn't feel better. At least they were cleaner. She patted them dry, and Patsy dotted them with ointment. Then she pulled on a pair of loose-fitting pajamas and eased herself to the bed.

"What's Jess doing?" she asked.

"He has the tractor and wagon in the field," Patsy said. Cassie knew he would be loading the bags and tire on that.

"Will you see if he needs help?" she asked.

"I will," Patsy said, "and I'll take care of the house too, if you promise to stay and rest."

Cassie didn't need persuading. "I will," she said, "I promise." Her sister went outside and Cassie was left alone. She'd be no good to anyone now. Besides the physical hurt, she felt quite humiliated too, and though at first she tried to deny them, dad's words kept coming back, ". . . before somebody gets killed." She'd almost accomplished that. If her legs had been caught, or her head. . . . She didn't even want to think about it. It could have been Jess too. That possibility made her even more sick. And if she had been killed, he would have been blamed. Dad was beginning to look quite wise. At least he understood the danger.

In a little while Cassie heard Jess go by with the tractor and wagon. Poor Jess. He got the raw end of everything. For him especially, she was glad her injuries were not serious. Finally some of the pain subsided and she went to sleep.

When Cassie woke, it was past lunch time. Jess was standing at the door. "I looked in on you earlier," he said, "but you were asleep. How are you feeling now?"

"Better."

"Let me see your leg."

Cassie started to sit up and hesitated. The stinging began again. Jess helped her up the rest of the way and inspected her leg. "Can you walk?"

"I think so." He helped her to her feet and she stepped gingerly.

"You're going to be sore for a while, Cass. I'm glad it's not your face."

"So am I." Cassie didn't know why, but she started to cry. Jess took her by the shoulders.

"Is there something more?" he asked.

"No, but I just feel awful inside, hurt and sick and. . . ."

"What kind of sick? Like you need to go to the doctor?"

"Not that kind, but when I think of what I did, and. . . ."

Her brother put his arm around her shoulder. "The scared kind. Forget it," he said. "We both learned something."

She reached for a tissue and blew her nose. "How's Stampede?"

"Unhurt, but she's scared too."

"Of what?" Cassie said.

"I don't know. Whatever it is, it'll just take time."

"And today didn't help."

"No, it didn't, but at least she didn't get physically hurt. The foal is due in about three weeks."

"Oh, Jess, and I thought she couldn't possibly pull all that."

"Well, come and eat. I'll help you to the kitchen."

Cassie stayed in bed the rest of the day, and there was lots of time to think. How grateful she was that the incident had turned out as it did. Stampede was back in the corral, Jess was OK, and she would heal. On the surface everything looked unchanged. No one would guess what had nearly taken place, especially if she kept her gravel burns covered. But Cassie knew that some things *had* changed. Mostly she felt differently about dad; he did know what he was talking about.

The next morning Cassie made herself move around. Patsy still did the household chores, but she walked around to limber herself a little. She wouldn't dare move like a complete zombie when her parents came home.

Late that evening mother and dad drove in. Cassie, Jess, and Patsy were watching tv, but they all got up and went to the door.

"Hi," Jess said. "How was your weekend?"

"Peaceful," mother said, laying her bag on the counter. "Very peaceful." Dad looked better too. "And yours?"

"Nothing is that peaceful around here," Patsy said, "but Jess didn't tease too much about the cooking." For once her sister had said the right thing.

"And we're glad to have you both home," Cassie said. She gave mother a kiss, and dad.

"It's what we all needed," mother said. "Now you girls get to bed. Tomorrow is another day."

Dad took her by the arm. "In the bag," he said,

pointing to her mother.

''Oh, yes,'' mother said. She opened it and handed each of the girls a tissue-wrapped gift. Patsy pulled hers open first.

''A curling iron,'' she squealed. ''Oh, mother, how did you know?''

''Dad decided,'' she said.

Then Cassie opened her box. There wasn't much weight. She folded the paper back, and there was a beautiful figurine, a delicate riding horse. She almost felt like crying. ''Thank you,'' she said, ''thank you both.''

Cassie went to her room and to bed, but first she put the horse on her dresser. It meant something, and she was awfully glad to have her parents home.

10
Rain and a Race

The next morning it was raining. Dad was smiling when he came in for breakfast. ''This is something else we needed,'' he said. ''Seed in the ground is one thing, but making it grow is another. Can't be done without rain.''

Cassie was glad for it too. Besides the growing part and dad feeling better, the fresh coolness gave her a better reason for long pants and sleeves. She hoped it lasted.

The rain did last. By the following morning the green grass of spring peeked through the dry of winter. There was a whole new smell outside, as if everything was new and alive and popping. It continued until the ground was well saturated. It kept Cassie inside too, and by mid-week she was awfully anxious to get out. Spring blossomed so quickly. A single day could turn everything from bare and brown to green and sprouting. If you happened to be inside that day, you could miss the whole event and she didn't want to miss anything.

Later in the week the rain stopped, and the sun shone down like a ball of fire drying the saturated soil around the farm. Reddish tulip spears peeked through the soft ground of the garden, and the bright green foliage of promised daffodils lifted eagerly upward.

On Saturday Cassie woke just as the sun was peeking through her east window. She jumped up quickly and pulled on her clothes, taking time to rub ointment over her leg and shoulder. The scabs were beginning to itch.

When she got outside Jess had already put Stampede in the corral. She was ignoring the hay and nibbling at the fresh grass along the fence. Cassie curbed her instinct to bounce right over and walked a little more sedately instead, but as soon as she got close to the corral Stampede lifted her tail and pawed at the soft earth. That horse! Spring hadn't changed her any.

Lightning was in the corral too, and he trotted over to where Cassie stood. Cassie pulled grass, fed him over the fence, and wondered what the next colt would be like. After that she decided to inspect the tree.

Cassie looked carefully at the old wound as she curled her toes around it. It ran the length of the trunk all the way to where an elbow protruded on the low side and it was slick and cleanly hollow, just as if it had been scraped out by a shovel or spoon. How could the tree keep growing? Cassie climbed above the wound and looked closely for signs of budding. Yes, they were coming. In spite of the wound, the old tree would leaf once more. It hadn't given up. Cassie liked that. But she didn't stay in the tree long. Mother came out to look at the garden, and Cassie slithered part way down the far side and dropped to the ground.

"I thought maybe we would begin working today," mother said looking around, "but the ground is too wet. We'll have to wait 'til next weekend."

That was all right with Cassie. Some things about the garden were OK, but working in it was not necessarily one of them. She finished her Saturday chores and both she and Patsy were free when Cassie saw Celine coming down the road toward their house. She was riding Thunder and leading Ramona behind.

"Want to go for another ride?" Celine asked when Cassie greeted her at the drive.

Remembering last weekend, Cassie couldn't help feeling a little reluctant. "My work is done. I guess I could go." She tucked her long hair behind one ear and looked at Patsy. "Do you want to?"

Her sister looked a little reluctant as well. Last week must have been on her mind too.

"Well, if you don't want to . . ." Celine began.

"We'll go," Cassie said.

"Then jump on." Celine shoved the reins at her, and Cassie handed them to Patsy.

"You handle her this time."

Patsy pushed them away. "You do it."

"Make up your mind." Celine snapped, one hand on her hip.

Cassie pulled the reins back. She put a bare foot in

the stirrup, but she felt a lot less confident than she had the other time. Patsy climbed on behind, and Cassie turned the horse around.

''Stay behind me,'' Celine reminded. Cassie didn't have any intention of barging ahead. Following Celine and Thunder, they clacked along the blacktop road until they came to the old trail again. Celine turned onto it, and Thunder's hooves left tracks in the soft, damp earth. ''Blacktop is hard on a horse's feet,'' she said, ''and I don't want them to run there anyway. Ramona might spook with passing traffic. But Thunder does need competition. See if you can pass me.'' She pulled her horse sharply around and gave her a smart slap on the flank. She bolted forward.

It was a challenge, and Cassie's reluctance left her. She leaned forward and tightened her knees against Ramona's sides. ''Come on, girl, let's see what you can do.''

Ramona's shoulder muscles tightened, her legs stretched forward, and Cassie felt the spirited surge of power beneath. Thunder already had a head start, but in no time Ramona was closing the gap. Cassie crouched more tightly to his neck. ''Go, girl, go if you can.'' Hooves pounded the soft earth beneath her.

''Slow down,'' Patsy screamed. But Cassie didn't slow Ramona down. The horse ahead hit a low spot. Flying mud kicked up and spattered them all over. Yet it didn't alter Ramona's stride or Cassie's urging. A few more rods and they were crowding Thunder.

The trail was narrow, and Celine hugged the middle. ''Go, Thunder, go,'' she yelled.

Cassie tried moving right. Celine moved right too.

There was standing water ahead. She plunged her horse straight through it. Mud blanketed Cassie completely, and Patsy was driving her head into her backbone. She pulled Ramona in and called it quits. She was covered with mud. So was Ramona, and she didn't deserve to be treated that way. Besides, there might have been a collision, and last week was still fresh in Cassie's mind. She ran a sleeve across her eyes and they both slid off the horse.

"What were you trying to do?" Patsy demanded. She sounded scared.

"Trying to pass Celine," Cassie said. "She invited me to."

Celine brought her horse to a halt too. She galloped back toward them, but as soon as she got nearer, she covered her mouth with her hand. "Oh, your face. You should see your face. It's a regular mud pack." The grin spread beyond her hand.

Cassie didn't grin back. She didn't think it was funny. She scraped a chunk from her face, and Celine wiped the grin from her face too. She made her eyes get real big. "S-a-a-y, you nearly caught me."

"Nearly?" Cassie blurted. "Why, if you'd given me half a chance. . . ."

Celine cut her off again. "Did your dad agree to let you have a horse?"

That stopped Cassie where she was. She quit scraping and glanced toward Patsy, but Patsy turned and pretended to be cleaning mud from her leg. She wasn't dirty at all.

"Well, did he?" Celine demanded.

Cassie hesitated. She spit once to clean her mouth

and make sure something would come out. ''No,'' she said, ''he didn't. He . . . he said we couldn't.''

''Couldn't? What a creep!''

Creep? Cassie felt her lower jaw drop open. She and dad had had their differences all right, but he was no creep. Mud and all, she straightened and stuck her chin out. ''He is not,'' she said.

''He is. Anybody who won't let *two* daughters have *one* horse is a great big creep.'' Celine gave the pink scarf an emphatic swish.

Cassie felt her blood start to boil. She wanted to yank off the pink scarf, throw it in the mud and stamp on it, but she didn't make a move. She just stood there.

Celine reached down and jerked the reins from her hand. ''I'm going home,'' she said. She galloped off on Thunder, and, held by the reins, Ramona galloped behind her.

11
Stampede's Foal

Cassie stared after Celine. ''If I was a horse,'' she said, ''I'd rather know a girl whose dad wouldn't let her have me, than be owned by one like her.'' She waited a minute. ''Are you mad at me too?''

Patsy shook her head. ''Celine shouldn't have asked you to pass, not when she didn't intend to let you.'' She started smiling a little. ''But you do look funny. Your face especially.''

''I feel funny too,'' Cassie said, ''like my plaster job is ready to crack.'' She bugged her eyes out and wiggled her nose in every direction.

Patsy started to giggle. Cassie did too. ''Isn't it crazy?'' she said. ''Celine's the one who worries about her face, and I get the mud pack.'' She scraped more of it away. ''But poor Ramona. She should belong to someone who wants her, not someone whose name was just pulled out of a hat.''

''I agree.'' Patsy helped Cassie clean her face, and they started for home. When they arrived, the yard was clear, but Cassie waited on the porch while Patsy checked to see if mother was anywhere else in sight. She wanted to avoid questions. When her sister signaled that the coast was clear, she hurried down the hall to the bathroom, removed the rest of the mud, put her pants and shirt in the hamper and pulled on the clean clothes Patsy brought her. As she finished dressing and looked from the window, she saw dad and her brother leaning against the corral fence looking at Stampede. Cassie grabbed her visor and hurried to where they were standing.

''She doesn't look quite ready to foal yet,'' dad was saying.

''I don't think so either,'' Jess answered, ''but from what I have marked on the calendar, another week ought to do it.''

''Can I watch?'' Cassie asked.

''You seldom see a colt born,'' Jess said. ''Dr. Woods told me. It's not like in the movies.''

''Don't you have to be real careful when it comes?''

Her brother answered again. ''We make sure the nostrils are clear, dry it good, check the navel, and see that the foal nurses right away. Those are the main things.''

Cassie had been talking mostly to Jess, only because it turned out that way, but then on purpose she turned to dad. ''Hi,'' she said softly.

''Hi,'' dad said. He smiled a little. Then he looked

at Stampede again. "Well, there's nothing more to do but wait. If the weather stays right we'll leave her outside. She'll have more room." He took his foot from the rail. "We'll start on the north fence next. I want it ready when the pasture is."

"Good idea," Jess answered. They left and Cassie stood there alone. She pulled down the visor and studied the big horse on the other side of the fence. My, Stampede was big, so big you hardly noticed she was about to give birth. She didn't look much different than she had all along, but, even if the foal was another stallion, that was something to look forward to.

Stampede seemed to be looking Cassie over too, but for once she wasn't doing anything unfriendly about it. Jess had said that horses were sometimes more docile right before foaling. "But after it comes," he said "look out." Cassie wasn't looking forward to that.

They stared at each other a long time. Neither Cassie nor Stampede made a move. Finally Cassie thought it was time. She dropped from the fence for some green grass, but before she could even snatch it up, Stampede whinnied a warning and pranced nervously in a circle. Cassie let the grass fall at her side.

When the girls boarded the bus Monday morning, Cassie saw Mary sitting alone near the back. She started toward her, and Patsy followed, but when they reached the seat, Mary's books were stacked neatly beside her.

"I'm saving this seat for Celine," Mary said. "Did she tell you? I bought Ramona."

"You bought Ramona?" The bus jerked ahead, and Cassie dropped into the seat in front. "Well," she said after a minute, "Ramona is a special horse. She deserves someone who appreciates her.'' She turned to the front and put her nose in a book, but she wasn't reading. To herself she was thinking, *It should have been me.*

That day Cassie felt all mixed up. She felt that way until Thursday morning when she woke to the jolt of her bedroom door being thrown wide open. Her brother poked his head inside.

''Cass,'' he whispered loudly, ''it's here. The foal is here.''

Cassie jumped straight up. She crashed into the door as she tried to pass through it, backed up, and was jumping from the porch steps before she was really awake. Jess was already back at the corral. He had towels, a bottle of antiseptic, and a scoop of mash in his hands. Inside Stampede was just beginning to raise her front shoulders from the ground.

''It still has the afterbirth on,'' he called. ''Hurry, but don't startle her.''

By that time Cassie was on the rail beside him. The big mare turned and unveiled the shivering bundle beside her, dark and quite still.

''Is it all right, Jess?''

Jess didn't answer her at first. The mare gave it a few licks and it twitched. ''That's it,'' he coached. ''Dry him up. Get him going.'' Another lick, and Cassie could see the rise and fall of the ribs. Air was entering his lungs. She grinned.

''I guess so,'' Jess said. He grinned back.

Patsy came to the fence too. She had taken time to dress. The foal threw its head up, and then, as if the weight was impossible to support, let it drop back to the ground.

"What is it?" Patsy asked.

Jess leaned way over the rail and swung one leg with him. Stampede barred her teeth and set her weight. He backed off. The little foal raised its head again, and in the next moment was struggling to its feet.

"Isn't it beautiful?" Cassie whispered.

"Beautiful?" Patsy said. "It's all nose and legs. I think it's ugly."

"Oh, wait. It's trying again. Look." The little colt swayed, steadied itself, and switched its tail. "O-o-o-h," Cassie cooed again.

Jess slipped into the corral, crouched near the rails and nodded to the feed scoop he had left near Cassie. "Distract her. There's a lot of blood coming from the navel."

Cassie saw it too. The underside was all stained red. She grabbed the mash and dropped into the corral as the colt fell again.

"Be careful," Patsy said.

Stampede saw Cassie. She charged, and Cassie dropped the feed and dove between the rails. She went through and Stampede stopped before she hit the fence. Her teeth were showing.

"Your baby has to be tended," Cassie said, regaining her feet.

The big mare noticed the feed and whiffed some into her mouth. In those few moments Jess had reached the new little horse, cleared its nostrils, poured antiseptic on the navel, and was outside the fence again. Stampede turned and ran back toward it, and Jess approached the girls from the outside. Dad had come out of the barn too, and hurried toward them.

"It's here," Cassie called to him. "The foal is here."

"And guess what?" Jess said. He was all smiles. "It's a filly."

A filly. Dad stopped hurrying. He took a few more steps to the fence and leaned on the top rail. "Well, what do you know. It's a filly."

"It was bleeding some," Jess said, "but Cass and I took care of it."

Cass and I. It's a filly. Cassie was dizzy from it all. She climbed on the rail next to dad and saw the filly blink shyly at her new and bright surroundings. "Can I stay home today, dad? Please, oh please, dad. Just today," she pleaded.

Dad looked at her, pajamas, bare feet and all, and then at the bent scoop tossed against the rail. "All right," he said, "just for today."

Cassie threw her arms around him and squeezed.

12
Sugar for Amber

In a matter of moments the brand new filly took a few stick-like steps and, reaching the corral fence, its muzzle searched the rails.

"That's not your mother," Jess said. "Turn around." Stampede nickered softly, and the filly, by grace of instinct, found her mother's udder. She nursed briefly. The bleeding from the navel had stopped.

"She didn't eat much," Cassie said.

"Colts don't," Jess explained. "They nurse often but only take a little each time. See? She's satisfied now." The stubby tail was whisking briskly.

Cassie grinned and hung over the rails to catch the details. There was a perfect white blaze running from the top of the filly's forehead all the way to her soft pink nose. Her coat still seemed quite dark, but with the help of Stampede's tongue and the warming sun that came out, it took on a fuzzy baby appearance and lightened a little. Oh, she was pretty.

Before long, Patsy left to get ready for school. Jess and dad went in for breakfast too, but Cassie wasn't hungry, and she wasn't going to school. She was staying with the filly. Only when the growl of the school bus met her ear, did Cassie realize she was still in her pajamas. She ran in to change and met Patsy coming out. "I'll tell you everything she does," Cassie said, "everything all day long. I promise." She started down the hall to the bedroom. "But don't say anything to Celine or Mary. They wouldn't think it was much anyway."

The minute her pajamas were traded for jeans, shirt, and visor, Cassie hurried to the corral fence again. It soon became obvious that the main requirements for the new life were food and rest, for either seemed to fill the colt with enough energy to accomplish the other. After nursing she would flop down looking like she would never rise again, but after a nap she was on her feet seaching for her mother. Stampede was never far away. Neither was Cassie, only she was on the other side of the fence.

Near noon the filly seemed to gain more strength, at least enough to take notice of additional surroundings. She had just wakened from napping, nursed, and stood blinking again when she found Cassie. Cassie didn't know if it was the yellow visor, the paisley sleeves of the red shirt, or the fact that she had been there all along, that attracted her attention, but anyway the filly found her. On legs spread wide she moved toward her. Cassie stayed perfectly still. The filly came a few more steps, and Cassie could see her eyes. They were a beautiful deep brown, full of softness and wonder. Her eyelashes were long and noticeable too, but the curiosity in her eyes was the most captivating thing. She looked like she wanted to find out about everything. She was perfectly dry too, and her short mane curled at her neck. Her tail started to go again, faster and faster until Cassie almost had to giggle.

The filly stepped stiffy closer, her pink nose poking the air. It looked so terribly velvety soft that Cassie wanted to reach right out and touch it, but close behind were the piercing eyes of her mother. She came closer, and Stampede trotted between them. She separated them, but she couldn't deter the filly's curiosity, for the little one stepped awkwardly beneath her and searched Cassie out again. That made Cassie smile, especially when it happened several times.

"How's the new one doing?" dad asked as he and Jess came toward the house for lunch.

"You should see her," Cassie said. "I think she likes me. At least she acts like it when she isn't eating or sleeping." She looked up at dad. "But that's most of the time."

Dad smiled too, and Cassie looked back at the foal. "What do you think we should name her?"

Dad put an elbow on the rail. "I think you would be a lot better at naming a horse than I. Have anything in mind?"

"How about Amber?" Cassie said. "It's a name I never thought of before, but when the sun shines on her coat like that, well, it seems right for her."

"Amber," dad said slowly. He drew the sounds way out. "Yes, I think that sounds all right. What about you, Jess?"

"Looks like an Amber to me," her brother said.

"Then that's it. Come on," dad said. "We'll have lunch and Amber can have a few minutes of privacy."

When Cassie went back outside, she put a sugar lump in her pocket. The filly was on her feet. She had more control, and somehow to Cassie she didn't seem much like Stampede at all, especially her legs. They were long, thin, and quite graceful. Her nose did seem a little big for the rest of her, but when she looked at Cassie with those big chestnut eyes, well, Cassie forgot about her nose being a little thick.

Cassie moved slowly toward the fence. The foal saw her, perked up her ears, and took a couple of steps. Stampede, who was eating some yards away, raised her head and whinnied, but Amber paid no attention at all. At the moment she was more curious than hungry. Jess came and stood beside Cassie.

"She doesn't look thick at all, Jess, not like Stampede, I mean," Cassie said. "Look at her legs, her back too." She thought a moment. "If I started early enough, do you suppose . . .?"

Jess grinned and shook his head. "You can't make anything out of that animal, Cass, that she isn't already. Amber won't be a riding horse. She'll be a draft horse, but if my guess is right, she'll be the most beautiful draft in the country. Right now, that'll have to be enough."

Just before Patsy came from school, Amber ventured the nearest she had come. Cassie had her hand out, and the sugar lump was in it. She opened it, and the soft, velvet muzzle poked forward, searching. The filly's lips bumped the sugar, and the taste did the rest. She thrust her nose into Cassie's hand.

Cassie grinned and drew her other hand all the way down the soft furry neck. For the moment she was content.

13 Cassie Makes a Friend

In the following days Cassie spent all the time she could at the corral. Each morning when she left for school she put a sugar lump in her pocket. When she came home she ran to the rails and held out her hand. Amber soon ran to greet her and shoved her muzzle into Cassie's hand. It was such fun to have Amber search one hand and then the other. She became very wise. If the hand was in a pocket, her soft nose wiggled between elbow and waist, and she lifted it out. Every day it made Cassie giggle. After the sugar fun, Cassie ran around outside the corral, and Amber ran around inside.

Within a week school was dismissed for the summer. Cassie passed to seventh grade, not with the style Patsy did—her card boasted three A's—but that part couldn't have concerned Cassie less. School was over and though she still didn't have a riding horse, she did have the whole summer to spend with the filly.

Every day Amber's legs grew stronger and her nature more curious. Every movement was accomplished at breakneck speed, and every day she poked her nose into more corners. On the day the cows were put to pasture for the first time, her ears stood up straight when she saw them round the corner of the machine shed. They grazed along the far side of the corral paying no attention whatever to Amber or the other horses. Amber, however, was very interested in them, and one step at a time she edged right to the fence. A very large cow near the fence too, stood winding her tongue around the tender grass. As Amber was about to poke her nose through the rails, the cow raised her head and let out a long, low, ''Mooo.''

The little filly shot straight in the air. She left the ground with all fours, bounced down the same way, and shot lickety-split for the other side of the corral. Her tail was almost left behind. Cassie fell on the ground rolling with laughter.

By the time Amber reached her, she had forgotten the scare and was only interested in Cassie's antics. She nudged Cassie through the fence as she lay on the ground. Cassie wiped a tear of laughter and sat up. ''You want to play? OK,'' she said. ''I'll get up and run, but I get tired more quickly than you do. You've got *four* legs. Besides, if you were of any real account, I could ride you and wouldn't get tired at all.''

With her days filled like that, Cassie's longing for a riding horse was eased. Amber was always ready to play. Sometimes she was ready before Cassie was and still eager when Cassie was worn out. Then the nudging wasn't quite such fun. Yet it made the time pass quickly. Even folding clothes was not quite the distasteful job it had been. Still she did miss riding Ramona, and she still wanted a horse, especially when she saw Celine and Mary go by and heard Ramona and Thunder's hooves clacking on the blacktop. Then Amber didn't seem quite so funny or quite so cute, and Cassie's legs felt more than tired from running—they felt completely worn out.

Still, after Celine and Mary disappeared, she was glad to have the little filly. Patsy didn't seem to bug her as much either. With the summer swimming, Patsy worried less about her face and hair. Cassie forgot about some things too, like climbing walls and falling off the corral fence. She didn't even climb the tree as much. She was more interested in watching Amber grow and develop, and in being friends with the little colt. If she could really train Amber well, dad might reconsider the riding horse after all. As soon as she could she asked Jess how to start the training.

''Buy a halter,'' her brother said, ''and when Amber comes to you, put it on.''

''What do you mean by that?'' Cassie asked.

''Patience,'' Jess said, ''time and patience. Don't force her. She'll let you know when she's ready. But with Amber, it won't take long. That little filly is so curious she'll poke her nose into anything you have.'' Cassie grinned.

''Once she has the halter on,'' Jess said, ''let her go. Then gradually get it around to where you're doing the leading. But it'll take patience.''

''What about Stampede?'' Cassie asked.

Jess turned toward the big animal. ''I don't think she'll be a problem. Where is she when you and Amber chase and act up now?''

Cassie thought a minute. ''She never comes around. On the other side of the corral, I guess. I haven't really noticed.''

''Notice,'' Jess said. ''I think she's accepted the fact that her wayward baby has chosen you for a friend. Notice, but casually, from the corner of your eye.''

''Will I have to take her out of the corral?''

''I wouldn't. Get in with her.''

''But Stampede. . . .''

''It'll be all right. You'll see. Besides, I want to be around the first time you try.''

''What about dad?''

''Don't worry about dad,'' Jess said. ''He'll see too.''

14 Training Begins

Cassie stood there a moment more, and something else crossed her mind. "Have you thought more of your plans for Arizona?" she asked.

"Yes, and no," Jess answered. "No, because I've been too busy to do anything specific, and yes, because it has to be sometime."

"So you do intend to go?"

"When the time is right. But people are like horses; some take longer, some shorter, but each needs his own time to accept or reject an idea."

The next time Cassie got to town she headed straight for the horse supply section at the farm store and chose a yellow, weanling halter. Amber wasn't weaned yet, but it was the smallest size available, and the color would accent the dark sorrel of the filly. She chose a time to try it when dad had gone to the field, but Jess was still in the house.

"Would you keep an eye on Stampede?" she asked her brother. "I'm going to give the halter a try."

"Sure," Jess said. "I'll stay on the porch unless I see trouble coming. If I do, I'll beat it over."

"Thanks," Cassie said. With the halter in one hand and a sugar lump in the other, she headed for the corral. Amber saw her coming, and, with tail flying, galloped right to the fence. This time Cassie didn't stop at the rails. She climbed to the top and dropped to the other side as if she had been doing it all her life. Stampede raised her head and switched her tail, but then turned away. Lightning trotted over to investigate, but he soon lost interest.

At first Amber seemed a little surprised. She pricked up her ears and gave a quick jump, but as soon as Cassie held out her hand, things were the same as they'd always been; Amber started searching.

The lump wasn't in the extended hand. That one held the halter, and she nosed it thoroughly before she tried the other. Then Cassie hung the halter on that one, but she also let the filly find the sugar. As soon as the sweets were gone, she nosed the halter again. Cassie had it hanging just right. The filly slid her nose into the front section, and Cassie slipped the strap over her ears and snapped the buckle. The halter was in place.

For a moment Amber stood a little stiffly. She gave her head a slight twitch, but before she had time to be spooked Cassie distracted her. "Come on," Cassie said, "let's run." She darted ahead, but didn't take hold of the halter. That was all the encouragement Amber needed. In two strides the filly was ahead of Cassie and moving out. Cassie stopped and Amber circled and came back.

''I'm too tired to run,'' Cassie said, putting her arms around her neck. ''Let's talk.'' She told her all about the day she was born, how they thought they would never have a filly, and what a surprise it was when she came. It was the first time Cassie and Amber had been so close, without at least a rail between them, and the young horse soaked up the closeness. It seemed to take some of the giddiness from her too, and before long Cassie took hold of the halter and they walked along together. When Cassie felt the filly becoming restless, she released her hold on the halter.

''So long, Amber,'' she said, ''I'll see you tomorrow.'' She climbed outside the rails. Amber kicked up her frisky heels, turned her head, and ran back to her mother to nurse.

''Couldn't ask for anything better than that,'' Jess said when she came toward the porch.

''No way,'' Cassie said, ''and Stampede didn't bother me at all.''

''She didn't bother,'' Jess said, ''but she didn't miss a trick either. She knew everything that was going on.''

''Really?''

He grinned. ''Sure. Horses look out of the corners of their eyes too.''

Every day after that Cassie spent time in the corral with Amber. First they always had a run to rid the filly of some energy. Then, when Cassie was tired or faked exhaustion, Amber settled down, Cassie hooked a rope to the halter, and they walked a while. Teaching her to start when Cassie wanted her to, stop when she was supposed to, and maintaining the right distance behind her was work, but it was pleasant work too. Besides, it might be very rewarding. Still, no matter what time of day Cassie went to the corral, dad never seemed to be around when she was there. She hoped he had noticed even though he never commented.

One evening toward the end of June an unusually fragrant odor tickled Cassie's nose as she was leaving the corral. A west breeze was blowing, and she thought it came from the garden where the flowers were. Leaving the halter rope on the ground, she went to see where it was coming from. In the first row she put her nose to the lemon fluff. It wasn't quite open, and there was no fragrance there. The lythrum was beginning to blossom too, but that did not smell much either. The flowering mint, of course, had a particular odor of its own, but that wasn't what she was looking for. She went further to where the first phlox had opened, but that wasn't it either. In fact, the fragrance was fading.

Cassie turned and started east again. It wasn't the raspberries. Their blossoms had already disappeared, yet on that side of the garden the fragrance grew stronger. She hurried back toward the corral, and passing the basswood tree, she glanced up. It was the sweetest, most delicate. . . . Cassie snatched a low hanging branch and brought it to her nose. It was the tree, laden with blossoms that were just beginning to unfold. Cassie had never seen it blossom before. She climbed it and leaned into the branches. It was heavenly.

In a short while dad came down the drive. He stopped at the corral and looked at the horses; and then started toward the garden too. Cassie watched him sniff the lemon fluff, the lythrum and others and start back toward the corral. She grinned. When he was right under the tree she broke a blossom, and, through the maze of leaves, dropped it smack on his head. "Hi," she said, and grinned down at him.

Dad looked up and smiled too.

"It's the tree," she said. "Isn't it something?" She hurried down and dropped the last few feet to where he was standing. "Did you know it blossomed like this? I didn't." She picked another blossom and brushed it under his nose.

"Neither did I," dad said, taking the blossom from her hand, "but I guess it's never too late to learn. Run and get mother."

Cassie ran to the house, and mother and Patsy came with her right away.

"It's an absolute marvel," mother said when she saw it. "The tree never has blossomed like this. Oh, I suppose there's some blossoming every year, but it's never been enough to notice. It's going to fill the whole area with fragrance."

"Look at it from here," Patsy said. She was on her knees by the trunk and looking upward. "It's turning a gold color.

Cassie knelt beside her. "Oh, it is." The blossoms hung heavily from the underside of the branches. She ran to get Jess too. She wanted to share the tree with everyone. Mother harvested some for making tea.

"I understand it's delicious," she said. "I read it somewhere, but I've never tried it." Cassie tried the tea, but preferred smelling the blossoms.

In the following days, they all made daily trips to the tree to watch its progress and inhale the fragrance. Cassie came more often than the others, however. She watched it turn from a delicate green to a deep, vivid gold. The whole family had picnics and visits under its shade, and Cassie began to feel a lot more comfortable with dad. Still, two weeks later when the blossoms finally faded to a light yellowish color, he still hadn't said one more thing about a riding horse or her training Amber in the corral.

15
First Day of School

The basswood tree had finished blossoming and Cassie was leading Amber one morning when she heard horses' hooves on the blacktop. Patsy was standing on the rails beside her.

"I bet it's Celine and Mary," Cassie said to her sister.

"Probably," Patsy said. "Jess heard the old trail has been widened. Maybe they can ride side by side now."

Celine came into view. She was riding Thunder, and behind her was Mary on Ramona. One glance and Cassie realized she had forgotten how beautiful those horses looked.

Patsy waved, and Mary waved back. Cassie waved too, but Celine just looked. Finally she smiled and raised her hand a little. Cassie didn't feel like smiling back. Was it the way Celine made her feel, or was it the horse she had and Cassie didn't?

Patsy nudged her and leaned close to her ear. "They have their hair cut," she whispered.

So they did. Both cuts were alike. The hair wasn't short, but it didn't touch the shoulders either. It was parted in the middle and curled around the face.

"It's the latest style," Patsy whispered again. Cassie didn't say anything or feel anything. For sure it wasn't the hair that bothered her.

That night when Cassie went to their bedroom, Patsy was already there. Dressed in her nightgown, she was sitting on the edge of the bed staring into space. Cassie flopped down and stretched out on her side.

"Should we get our hair cut?" Patsy asked.

Cassie looked at her sister a minute. "I don't really want mine cut," she said, "but if you want yours done, go ahead. Do you think you'd look better that way?"

Patsy stood in front of the mirror and wadded her hair shorter on the sides. She tilted her chin and scrinched her nose a little. "Not really," she answered.

"Do you think you'd like it better if it was shorter?"

She tilted her chin the other way. "Probably not."

"Will it be easier to take care of?"

"I don't think so."

"Then why cut it?" Cassie asked.

Patsy let her hair drop and flopped on her bed. "It looks OK on Celine, but. . . ." She rolled over and came up with elbows propped on the bed. "I don't really like the way she acts."

"Neither do I," Cassie said. But she did like her horse, and she did like Ramona.

The rest of the summer was spent working with Amber. Cassie did enjoy the friendship and the antics of the filly, and she tried to be satisfied. Yet she couldn't dispel the quiet wisps of regret. Spring had come, the best time for a horse, but it had passed without one.

Yet the progress of the filly gave her cause for satisfaction. Amber had learned quite well how far to stay behind Cassie when she was led. She knew she was to start at, "Giddap," or a soft click of the tongue, and to stop at, "Whoa." And, lately, dad had come to the corral and watched the training too. If it had been out of the corner of his eye a few weeks ago, it wasn't any more.

Cassie put school out of her mind as long as she could. Finally, she had to face its starting, but she was far from overjoyed. She hated wearing shoes again. Besides, there was also the prospect of having to deal with Celine every day. Celine had a knack for saying the most irritating things. And Cassie knew she couldn't avoid her. Trying to do so would be too obvious.

On the first day of school, Celine had apparently spent the night at Mary's since they were both on the bus when Cassie and Patsy boarded. They were sitting near the back, and Cassie walked right up to them.

"Hi," she said. "I see you both have your hair cut. It looks nice."

Mary smiled a little and flipped her hair to one side. She was acting more like Celine every day.

Celine smoothed hers a little too. "Thank you," she said coolly. "You two don't look much different."

Cassie shrugged. She felt different inside, but maybe

it didn't show.

Another problem with school was that it ended the leisure of summer, and though Cassie wouldn't say it to Celine or Mary, she missed her time with Amber. Yet she always took her sugar lump, and, every afternoon, no matter how briefly, she and Amber had their daily session with the sugar lump and romp. It was the one truly bright spot in her life.

But Cassie liked the weather too, dry, crisp, and cool. Soon the leaves started to turn from their summer green to the red, yellow, and orange of fall. The horses, having been outside most of the summer, except on nights when it rained, were put inside again. Lightning was taken to the barn, but Stampede was tied in a small shed so there would be room for Amber beside her. She was still nursing. The little filly wasn't tied, for once darkness came, she never strayed far from her mother.

On the last Friday in September, Cassie woke to the first frost of the season. That brought with it an urgency to get everything done before winter. It was the whole topic of conversation at breakfast.

''The weatherman promises a good day for tomorrow,'' mother said, ''and it will be busy. The potatoes must be dug and put away. Carrots too. Then we'll till the garden so that it will be ready to cover with leaves when they fall.''

''That won't be long,'' Jess said. ''Not after this frost.''

Dad drank the last of his coffee. ''We'll finish the silo filling and start picking corn. The horses need deworming too.'

''What for?'' Cassie asked.

"To get rid of parasites," Jess answered. "We'll take care of that tomorrow too. I'll get the medicine in town today."

"I want to get bedspreads and blankets washed too," mother said, "and hang them out. It may be the last nice day for a while."

Cassie was glad to leave for school. The talk alone was wearing her out.

By mid-morning the sun had burned the frost from the ground—warming the day and blazing in the red and orange maples of the school grounds. Cassie was eager to be in the open. When the dismissal bell rang she dashed for the bus, hung her head as far out the window as she dared, and enjoyed the warmth and color all the way home. It might be the last nice day of the season.

When the bus stopped, Amber was waiting at the fence. Seeing Cassie, she reared up on her hind legs, and nickered softly. One front hoof rested momentarily on the rail. Her fuzzy coat glistened in the sunlight, and she looked more like a pleading puppy than a growing filly. Cassie jumped into the corral and grabbed the filly around the neck. "Come on," she said, "we'll have a good time tonight."

Cassie started to run, but Amber bunted her hands and chest.

"Oh, you want your sugar first. OK, where is it?" Cassie put both hands in her pockets, closed them, and pulled them out.

Amber sniffed both hands then chose one. Her nose and lips worked and nudged until Cassie opened her hand. The lump was there.

"Sure enough," Cassie squealed, "you picked the right one tonight." And Amber tossed her head, showed her teeth, and nickered again.

"Come on," Cassie said. She grabbed the rope from the fence, snapped it to the halter, and left the corral for the open pasture. This was a special day, and they would have one last fling before the onset of winter.

At first Cassie let Amber run in the open space. And run she did. Cassie didn't even try to keep up. She darted at random too, feeling the wind on her face and legs. When Amber tired of being by herself she galloped back, teased a little, and headed in another direction. Finally, Amber had enough running and trotted back, and Cassie hooked the rope to the halter.

"Look at those leaves," she said, "all red and gold and that little green pine to set them off. See? Right over there." She pointed and swung out of the way for a better view.

Amber followed eagerly. A soft nicker, a gentle nudge, and they were on their way again parading the pasture.

"There's the cranberry swamp," Cassie said, and remembered she hadn't gathered any. "We'll get those tomorrow," she added, "if the frost doesn't have them already. But they're for me. You won't like them as well as you like sugar."

Amber seemed to understand. She rubbed her neck against Cassie's arm and the velvet nose touched her cheek. The brown eyes looked into Cassie's and the horse nickered softly.

Cassie felt a wave of real love ripple clear through her, and she put her arms around the filly's neck.

Amber was more than a colt. She was a wonderful precious friend.

Just then mother called from the house. ''Cassie, come for supper.'' Cassie hated to leave, she hated to see that afternoon end, but she knew it was time.

''I'm coming,'' she called, and the girl and her horse walked home together.

16
Too Much to Do

When Cassie came into the house, everyone was already eating at the kitchen table.

"Where have you been?" mother asked. "I've been calling and calling."

"In the pasture with Amber," she said. "I didn't know it was so late." She slid into her chair.

"Eat right way," mother said. "As soon as you're finished I want you to take the carrot bins from the basement and fill them with sand. You can use the sand in the bags behind the shed. The old wagon in the garage will work for hauling them." She nodded toward the coffee pot, and Cassie poured more for dad. "You'll have to fill several. Patsy, you get the potato bins ready."

"Do we have to wash them?" Patsy asked.

"The potatoes?" mother said. "Of course. I don't like to put them in the sink all covered with soil. It plugs the drain. But if the bins are ready, we'll be set for an early start in the morning."

Cassie sighed a little. Getting ready for winter was not nearly as much fun as playing with Amber.

Dad turned to Jess. "Right after chores," he said, "I'll blow that last load into the silo and you can start mounting the picker. Did you get the dewormer?"

Jess nodded. "Right there on the counter."

"Good. Cassie can take care of that in the morning too."

"Should I do it tonight?" Cassie asked.

"The bins," mother reminded.

"No," Jess said. "I'm putting the horses in now, and they have to be separated so that each one gets the right amount. Do it in the morning."

Cassie finished supper, changed clothes, and hurried to fill the bins, but she had to push herself. All signs indicated a hurried weekend.

It seemed awfully early when mother called in the morning. "Bring your sheets and blankets," she said. "We're doing all the bedding today."

Cassie stumbled to her feet, wadded everything from the bed in one roll, and made her way to the kitchen. Patsy came behind her. Jess and dad were eating breakfast. If they were already done with the morning chores, it wasn't as early as she had thought.

"Put those things by the washer," mother said. "One load is ready for the line now. Then come and eat."

Cassie dropped her bundle in the empty basket and went to the table. Mother was just bringing the bacon and eggs.

"It's going to be good drying outside," she said. "and if there's extra time, a few more windows need doing." Cassie dropped into the chair next to dad with a little inward sigh. The chores seemed endless.

"Two days should take care of the corn picking," dad said. He passed the serving plate to Jess. "Get together what you need for that." They had swallowed their food and were on their way out before Cassie even started eating. At the counter Jess paused and picked up the can of dewormer.

"I'm putting the horses out right away," he said. "This stuff goes by weight. Let's see, it'll be five tablespoons for Stampede, three for Lightning, and one for Amber. I'll tie Lightning at one end of the corral and Stampede at the other, and you can take care of Amber." He set down the can. "But do it right away so that I can turn them loose before I go to pick."

Cassie was finally starting to wake up. She shoved in the first forkful. "OK, I'll do it right away."

Mother was already clearing the table. "Take those wet things with you and hang them up. I need the basket for another load."

"OK," Cassie said. She finished her eggs and toast, picked up the can of dewormer, and read the directions. One tablespoon for every 400 pounds. Yes, that would make it right. As she closed the door, Jess was tying Lightning to one rail.

"Do it right away," he said again.

Hurry, hurry, hurry. "I'm coming," Cassie said.

Amber met her at the rails and nudged the can in her hands. "No sugar this time of day," Cassie said. "You have to wait." She opened the can and gave Lightning three spoonfuls. Amber tried mouthing the can. "This isn't for you," Cassie said. "Come on. You'll get yours."

Jess tied Stampede and Cassie climbed outside the rails and reached through them. Stampede didn't make a fuss, but she did back up.

"Five for you," Cassie watched from the corner of her eye while she scooped it out. Amber went after the can again.

"Boy, you really want to play.' Cassie went a couple more lengths and climbed inside again. She intended to serve Amber's share and watch her until all were done, but Amber hadn't followed. She was licking Stampede's portion.

"Hey, come here." Cassie held out the can to lure her. Amber kicked up her heels, charged over and knocked it from her hand. All the contents spilled on the ground. She started licking that too.

"Here," Cassie cried, grasping the halter and raising her head. "You can't have all that. It's enough for a dozen horses your size."

Jess started coming back.

Cassie looked around for something to clean it up, but there was nothing at hand. "Last night really got her going," she said to her brother. "Listen, will you hold her while I. . . ."

"Jess!" It was dad calling from the silo.

"I have to go," he said.

"Can I tie her?" Cassie asked.

"If it's only for a minute. She'll have to learn anyway. Weaning time's not far away."

The rope was draped on the fence. Cassie fastened

one end of it to the fence and the other to the halter so that Amber couldn't reach the spilled dewormer and jumped the rails. "I'll only be a minute," she said.

Amber wasn't listening. Even if she was, she was in no mood to be left alone. Coming to the end of the rope, she kicked her heels in the air, and nickered loudly.

"I'll only be a minute," Cassie said again. She hurried toward the house, but Amber kept on making a fuss. She was flinging her head, twisting her body, and straining against the rope. Stampede started pawing too. Dust rose around her.

Cassie ran ahead anyway. Inside she grabbed the dust pan and whisk broom and mother called from the other room.

"You forgot the wet things."

Cassie turned, re-arranged the things in her hand, and took the basket too. She was on her way out when she glanced from the window and saw Celine and Mary on the road. Their horses pranced in perfect precision, heads poised, tails lifted, and coats polished to a high luster. And Celine and Mary—like two peacocks they perched aloof in the saddles. Every hair was in place, everything matched. They even wore gloves. Suddenly Cassie felt terribly exhausted. She could hear Amber whinnying louder than ever, but she couldn't face those two again, not right now. She let the door slip closed.

17
The Accident

Cassie waited, a little twinge of guilt growing inside as she heard Amber fussing in the corral. When she looked out the door again Mary and Celine had passed. She gathered the things and opened the door in time to see Amber kick her hind legs again. They were toward the fence, and as she thrust them outward, one shot through the small space where the offset rails met. It was trapped, and for a moment the back end of the filly hung there. Then Cassie heard a crack, and Amber whinnied loudly. Dropping the broom and basket, Cassie raced to the fence.

The leg slipped free and Amber crumpled to the ground.

"Jess! Jess!" Cassie screamed. She jumped over the rails and dropped to the ground beside the fallen animal.

In a moment dad and Jess were beside her. Mother

and Patsy were there too.

"What happened?" Jess asked.

Tears blurred Cassie's vision. It was hard to speak. "Amber was kicking. I was only going to be gone a minute." She pointed to the place where the rails overlapped. "Her leg got caught right there."

Amber was quiet. Jess untied the rope, and Cassie lifted the still head to her lap. The filly didn't nudge. She didn't bunt her hand for sugar. Even her eyes looked different.

"Amber spilled the stuff, and I had to leave," Jess explained. "I told Cassie to tie her." He carefully lifted the leg, and Cassie felt a tremor pass through the small body.

"Patsy, call Dr. Woods," Jess said. "I think it's broken." His words sent a creeping numbness into Cassie's heart. When Patsy was gone, everyone just stood there.

Finally mother put a hand on Cassie's shoulder. "I'm so sorry," she said.

In a few minutes Patsy was back, and a short while later the veterinarian backed his truck to the fence and stepped out.

"There's been an accident," Jess said. "the filly kicked and caught her leg in the fence. I think it's broken."

Dr. Woods looked at dad and then at Cassie who was still holding Amber's head. Then he knelt down, and with careful pressure examined the leg all the way from the ankle to the hip. He moved it gingerly. Amber trembled again, and Cassie held her closer.

Finally Dr. Woods sat back and pushed the cap from

his forehead. "You're right," he said, "it's broken."

"Is there anything we can do?" Jess was on his knees too.

Dr. Woods shook his head. "Not a thing. If it was the lower leg, I might give you some encouragement, but it's the hip—a bad break.

"But it can't be," Cassie wailed softly. "She caught the *end* of her leg."

"I don't doubt that," Dr. Woods said, "but the pressure and the twist came above. I'm sorry."

Dad took the cap from his head and said wearily, "Well, I guess we don't have any other choice."

"No," Cassie cried. "I won't let you kill her. I won't, I won't."

"Isn't there something . . . ?" Jess pleaded.

Dr. Woods stood up and closed his bag. "It only prolongs the agony," he said.

"I won't, I won't," Cassie cried again. She hung onto the filly's neck sobbing, but she kept hearing over and over the dreadful finality in her father's voice.

The next hours were a nightmare. No one and no place could comfort Cassie. She wanted to protect Amber, to go and run with her in the fields, to start the day over again, anything to change what had happened. But there was nothing she could do and her utter helplessness drove her wild. It was evening before she quieted down and could begin to think at all. She was lying in her room because she had to be somewhere when mother came in and sat quietly on the bed.

"It's very hard to accept what's happened," she said. "Amber was not an ordinary filly. She was a vital, precious creature. You loved her, and you are very, very sad.''

''Oh, I am,'' Cassie wailed. ''Oh, mother, after I tied Amber I saw Celine and Mary on the road and I waited inside till they passed because I just couldn't face them. If only I hadn't waited.'' She started to cry all over again, but this time she let her mother hold her.

''Well dear, we all have our 'if only's,' '' mother said when Cassie had quieted down. ''Jess said 'if only' he had helped you. And 'if only' I hadn't stopped you for the wet laundry. But then, maybe none of our 'if only's' would have made any difference. 'If only's' can't change what's happened, so we shouldn't let them worry us.''

Cassie was quiet for a while. Then she said, ''I'm going to miss Amber so much. She would wait for me after school, and I used to tell her things.''

''She was a special horse, wasn't she,'' said mother. She patted Cassie's cheek, ''Supper will be ready in a few minutes. Why don't you wash up and come join us. We'll all feel better if you do.''

That night Cassie could not get to sleep. She lay awake thinking all sorts of things. She wished she had been able to forget about the horse she thought she had to have. It didn't seem important anymore. She wished she could have forgotten about Celine and Mary and their horses. She wished she could still be training Amber. She wished she still had her for a friend. But most of all she wished she had been satisfied with her alone.

18
Stampede Makes a Friend

Finally Cassie drifted off to sleep. Yet many times she woke and thought she heard a lonesome whinny in the distance.

In the morning Jess came to tell her he had prepared a place beneath an oak in the pasture. It was where she and Amber had romped the night before. Though it hurt again, Cassie tried to thank him. Thoughtful Jess. He had always been her friend.

At breakfast Cassie was sure she heard another whinny. Dad was beside her. He didn't say anything, but he reached over and filled her glass with milk. He poured his own coffee too, and passed the platter.

"You'd better have another egg," he said.

Cassie couldn't swallow another egg. She could hardly take her eyes from the table, but she did know dad was trying to tell her something. Cassie wanted to tell him things too, like wishing she'd been satisfied with Amber even if she never got a horse, but they wouldn't come out.

When the meal was over, Cassie went to her room again and stood looking from the window. Jess brought the horses to the corral. Lightning seemed the same, but when he let Stampede go, she whinnied and tried to go back through the gate. Jess closed it. She put her tail in the air, made a complete circle back to the gate and whinnied again. She kept looking over the fence.

Cassie stayed inside all afternoon, but every so often she heard that lonesome whinny, and whenever she looked from the window, Stampede was either running from one end of the corral to the other or holding her head in the air searching. She didn't lower it even to eat.

On Monday and Tuesday Cassie avoided the corral though she did go to school. She had to, but she stayed away from Celine and Mary too, not because she blamed them for anything, but because she hadn't had the courage to say, "Amber may not be what you want, or even what I want, but for what she is, I love her anyway." They didn't say anything to her either. Yet Cassie was sure they knew, for she heard Patsy talking with some of the others in Mrs. Milford's class.

When she awoke on Wednesday it was cold in the house. The sky was gray and overcast, and a blustery wind was blowing the leaves from the trees. Cassie had breakfast and buttoned her brown, wool sweater tightly around her. As she passed the table on her way to meet the bus, her hand, mostly out of habit, reached for the sugar bowl. She paused a moment, then slipped a lump in her pocket and closed the door behind her.

All day Cassie felt very alone. The sky remained overcast and gloomy, and the ride home was the same. At the drive, Patsy left the bus before she did. As Cassie began the lonely walk to the house, she looked toward the corral. Stampede gave another whinny. Nervously she trotted back and forth. She tossed her head and pawed a little, but somehow the trot didn't seem malicious like it had before, and the pawing was more pleading than defiant. Mostly it looked distressed.

Cassie's heart went out to the great animal. Poor thing. She missed her baby too. Walking to the fence, Cassie rested her head on her arms. A few more tears soaked the brown, wool sweater, but the tears were not for herself. They were for Stampede. The big Belgian had never chosen to be her friend, yet if she ever needed one, it was now. Still Cassie couldn't decide for her, but she *could* be there.

With her head in her arms, Cassie stayed, neither thinking, hearing, nor speaking, lost in thought. Then, something touched her hand. It felt gentle, tender, caring, like a soft velvet nose. She raised her head, and across the rails Stampede's brown eyes gazed into hers.

Cassie reached in her pocket and held out the sugar lump. She didn't coax or tease, she didn't urge, but simply offered.

For only a moment or so Stampede hestitated a little. Then she shifted her weight and cautiously edged her nose to the sugar lump. The large, soft lips carefully worked it between her teeth. Finally there was a delicate crunch, and in another moment Stampede was nuzzling Cassie's hand almost the way Amber did.

Cassie felt a mixture of sadness and joy—sadness because the loss was so great for both of them, joy because it helped so much to share it. But mostly she felt the same warm feeling she had known before, the comfort of friendship.

In the following days that friendship meant more to Cassie than even she had thought it would, and every afternoon she hurried from the bus to the corral with her lump of sugar. At first Stampede was cautious, but as the days passed and the last leaves of autumn fell from the trees the great horse began to wait for Cassie and would nicker a greeting. Cassie began stroking her soft nose and patting the huge neck. After a while, Stampede seemed to welcome the caresses.

One gray afternoon when Stampede seemed more friendly than usual, Cassie climbed up the rails and ran her hand down the thick sturdy neck. She leaned over and put her arms around it, and the next thing she knew she was on Stampede's back. There was no saddle, no blanket, no reins, just a big broad back, but it was steady. Cassie laid Stampede's mane to the right and the skin rippled over her flesh. Did she dare? She took hold of the heavy mane, gave a gentle signal with her tongue, and the big Belgian mare moved ahead.

Cassie was still riding when dad came home. He stopped the truck and walked right to the corral. At the same time Jess started toward her from near the barn.

Cassie smiled at both as she neared them. She stopped Stampede and waved from across the fence.

Jess kept coming. He smiled too. In fact, he was grinning, but dad just looked bewildered.

"I never would have believed it," he said.

"I tried gee and haw," Cassie said. "She knows everything." She glanced at her brother. "She can pull too. We know that."

Dad still didn't say anything.

"I could help you on Saturdays," Cassie went on. "If you hooked the logs, I'd ride her out. I'll bet she'd behave then." She patted Stampede on the neck. "But you'd have to harness her. I can't lift that."

Dad still didn't say much more, only, "I never would have believed it."

Cassie rode Stampede around a little longer. The next day she rode her again, not only because she and Stampede were friends, but to show dad the whole thing was really true. He hadn't been dreaming. When Jess was done with his other work, he brought the harness to where they were, and Cassie talked to Stampede while he put it on. She had extra sugar in her pocket in case she needed it, but she didn't. The only time the big horse fidgeted a little Cassie stroked her nose and cooed, "There, girl. There, girl." Jess said soothing words too, and she settled down right away.

When all the harness was strapped and buckled, Jess helped Cassie onto the Belgian's back again and held the singletree while they walked over to where dad was standing.

"See?" Cassie said. "I'll be on her like this while you hook the logs. Watch. Back, girl," she said, "back a little.''

Jess was still holding the singletree, and Stampede took a few steps backward.

Dad shook his head.

''When you're done,'' Cassie said, ''I'll ride her out and unhook. Do you think that will work?''

Dad was still shaking his head, but he smiled too. ''Yes, Cass,'' he said. ''It just might work.''

19 New Beginnings

Cassie had always hoped that she and Stampede could be friends, and finally, even though it came about in a way she wouldn't have chosen, it *had* happened. It was particularly comforting to know that the big draft horse was just as gentle as the filly.

That fall too, as dad and Jess finished the silo filling, the corn picking and other preparing-for-winter chores, things seemed to go better between them. At least dad would sit a little longer at the table and visit a little more, and the work didn't seem quite as frenzied.

When Cassie came downstairs for breakfast one Saturday, Jess and dad were already at the table. Mother was in the kitchen too, finishing the pancakes. Patsy came in, and for once they all ate a rather leisurely breakfast.

When everyone had finished, Jess leaned back in his chair, looked outside a while and then back at the others. "Feels really good to have everything secured and ready for winter," he said. Cassie knew he was talking about the full silo and corn crib.

"It does," dad said, "it really does." He took his cup by the handle, and turning it back and forth on the saucer, watched the liquid moving inside. "I've been thinking, Jess," he said finally, still watching the coffee, "since that's all done, and Cassie has offered to help me in the woods on Saturdays,"—his voice sounded a little shaky—"if you still have it in mind to see some of the country, this might be the time for you to do it."

Cassie felt a little jump of surprise inside her. She glanced over at Jess, and he looked surprised too. For just a second she feared his chair might tip backward, but then he took hold of the table and leaned forward. He glanced toward her, and Cassie gave him a smile of encouragement. Jess deserved to go. He always worked so hard. She was awfully glad things were working out.

"I appreciate that," her brother said. "This . . . this would be a good time." Cassie could see the excitement in his eyes. "I can be ready to leave in a few days."

The family had fun helping Jess get his things ready for the trip, but for the first time Cassie could remember, her brother was disorganized. He didn't know where to start, but she and the others took over.

"You'll need a tent," Cassie said, "a camp stove, cooler, and a sleeping bag."

He started a list.

''One frying pan and a boiling pan,'' mother said.

''And a big thermos jug,'' Patsy added, ''especially if you're going to the desert.'' Cassie wondered if he was going to the desert, or the mountains, or Arizona, but she didn't ask.

''I guess it's not so much *where*,'' Jess said, ''but more a question of time and room.''

''Better take oil,'' dad said. ''That truck isn't as new as it once was.''

''I will, dad. Thanks.''

Cassie helped her brother organize a box of maps. There was one for just about anywhere that could be reached by car. She even supplied him with writing material, because she wanted to know all about his experiences.

''Take plenty of pictures too,'' she said. ''I don't want to miss a thing.''

On the day Jess was to leave, Cassie and Patsy went to school as usual, only Cassie swung past the corral to greet Stampede before she boarded the bus. She had started doing that each morning since they had become friends. Her brother planned to pack his truck during the day and be ready to leave when the girls returned in the afternoon. It would be their chance to give him a royal farewell.

That day Celine was not in school.

''I think her father is coming home,'' Mary said. ''That is, if he doesn't disappoint her again.''

The afternoon turned out to be beautiful, crisp and

clear. A tingling vitality seemed to fill the air, maybe because it was the day of her brother's beginning venture. Cassie felt it all the way home. What a grand day for Jess to be starting.

As the bus neared their drive, Cassie bent to get her books. With a quick goodby to Mary, she and Patsy started down the steps. On the last one she looked to see if Jess's truck was still there. It was, but she really didn't see it, for something else was there too, something that stopped her right where she was.

Near the truck was a horse, a beautiful, wonderful, unbelieveable horse. Patsy nudged her, and, stiff-legged, she dropped from the step.

Dad was holding the horse by the halter, and Jess was tightening the saddle. Mother was there too. They were all smiling.

The automatic closer drew the door from Cassie's hand. She managed one awkward step forward, and her legs began working again. She ran to where everyone was standing and drew her hand along the silky front shoulder. The horse was a sleek, lustrous chestnut—a rich cinnamon color—with small, pointed ears, clear, patient eyes, and on its slender neck was a softly falling mane. It was red.

"She's yours," dad said, handing her the reins.

Cassie stood there staring. "She's beautiful," she kept repeating, "just beautiful." It was all she could say.

"Aren't you going to ride her?" Jess asked at last.

"Sure," Cassie said. Dropping her books where she was, she put her foot in the stirrup. Then she took it out. "Just a minute," she said, and running to the fence she gave Stampede her sugar lump. "I'll ride you too," she promised, "every day." She ran back to the horse Jess held and settled herself in the smooth, leather saddle. "Will you go with me, Patsy?"

Her sister didn't wait for another invitation. She climbed on behind, and dad took his hand from the halter. "What will you name her?" he asked.

Mother patted dad's shoulder. "There's plenty of time for that later," she said.

"Her name is Cinnamon," Cassie said softly. It seemed the most natural thing in the world. *Her horse.*

Mother was smiling too, that same knowing smile she had every time some dream came to be. Cassie grinned at her. They knew it all along, God and her mother.

She nudged Cinnamon who started forward, her mane lifting in the breeze. It puffed a little, billowed, and settled down for the next rise. Her hooves clacked just right too. In fact, Cinnamon couldn't have been more grand if Cassie had handpicked the horse herself from the whole wild west.

Up the road a ways, Cassie turned onto the old but widened trail—and saw Celine. She was riding Thunder, but her head was down, and her shoulders were drooping. It looked like she had been crying.

Cinnamon nickered at Thunder, and, hearing the sound, Celine looked up. When she saw them, she whirled Thunder around and started her galloping off down the trail.

"Celine! Wait!" cried Cassie. And without thinking she nudged Cinnamon with her heels and gave her free rein. With a leap that almost unseated Patsy, Cinnamon jumped forward and in a moment had hit a long, reaching gallop. Cassie was caught up in the exhilaration of the run, the wind whipping by, and the red mane flying in front. They began gaining on Thunder slowly but surely.

"Celine! Please stop," Cassie called again.

Celine looked back, then began slowing Thunder. As Cassie and Patsy pulled to a stop beside her, she said in a sharp and defiant voice, "Well! Whose horse have you borrowed this time?"

Cassie was about to make a snappy retort, but suddenly saw the pain in her friend's eyes. She checked herself. "Cinnamon's mine," she said. "Dad bought him for me as a surprise. I just got him today."

She hestitated, then went on, "Say. I heard your dad came home today."

Celine looked down and rubbed the reins. "No," she muttered. "He . . . he couldn't make it again."

"Oh, I'm sorry," Cassie said. Celine shrugged, but didn't look up.

"Why don't you come over for supper tonight?" Cassie asked. "Then we can talk about horses."

"Oh, could I?" Celine perked up a little. "I'd like that." She gave her hair a little flip. For some reason it didn't irritate Cassie the way it usually did.

As they turned their horses to ride back down the trail, Cassie had a sudden wave of affection for her dad. Much as she loved Cinnamon already, she could see now that there were some things more important than having a horse.

"Hey, let's race," yelled Celine.

Immediately the two horses, feeling their owners' excitement, took off down the trail.